Warrior
of the
Egyptian Kingdom

Stephanie Jefferson

∞

Beyond Beyond Books

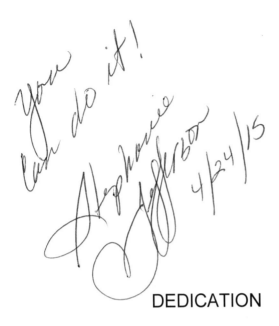

You can do it!

Stephanie Jefferson 4/24/15

DEDICATION

For my grandchildren—always. For my daughter who encourages me. For my husband—my hero, my heart. To the reality of determination and discipline that every girl must develop—Girl Power!

Warrior of the Egyptian Kingdom

ACKNOWLEDGMENTS

First, allow me to offer thanks, gratitude, and appreciation to my hard-working critique group and my wonderful beta readers, whose diligence I cannot do without. I would like to credit the title of this book to Carrie Malinowski. Her imagination and understanding of PRINCESS KANDAKE gave birth to the perfect title for this book. I must acknowledge the patience and support of my wonderful husband and family, without them none of this would be possible.

Cover
This beautiful cover was designed by Donna Casey. She can be found at digitaldonna.com. The photography for the cover was done by the talented eye and shutter of Tamona Kelly-Kreidl. Many thanks to them both.

1

Kandake walked from the entrance of the palace courtyard. Before she could get beyond it, her ears were assailed by her favorite sound—the laughter of children. A group of them playing a game of chase circled her with squeals of joy while one hid behind her skirts.

The vibration of hooves pounding the ground entered her feet at the same time the clatter reached her ears. A horse, moving at full gallop, came at the small group. Kandake whisked her small friends aside, out of the animal's path like a hen gathering her young. But one of her young chicks dropped his sweet treat and darted back to retrieve it. He bent over to pick it up right where the horse's hooves would strike next.

Kandake dove for the child. She tucked him into her middle and rolled them both to the least dangerous spot. The warrior atop the beast leaned forward, urged the animal into a leap. A whisper of air flashed across Kandake's cheek as the horse passed over her. Gravel sprayed her face when it landed.

The Nubian warrior vaulted from the horse's back. His feet hit the ground as he folded his body into a show of respect that placed his head near to the dusty ground. "Princess Kandake, I beg your pardon. I did not see you or the child."

"What brings you to the palace at such a pace?" she asked. Kandake laid her hand on the back of the warrior's head extending her pardon and allowing him to rise.

"I carry a message for King Amani from the pharaoh of Egypt."

"Then you must complete your mission." Kandake took the reins of the horse and urged the man to continue toward the palace. She called a servant to her and handed her the reins of the lathered beast. "Please take this warrior's horse to the compound. See that it is fed, watered, and rubbed down."

Kandake followed the warrior to find out what news had come of their northern neighbor and the Nubian warriors assisting Egypt's army. As she entered the throne room, she saw the warrior kneeling and proffering a packet of papers toward her father.

"My King," the warrior said, "an important message from Egypt's pharaoh."

Princess Alodia, the king's sister and advisor, accepted the message from the warrior's hand. She unfurled the hide that bound the pages and read its contents. "My King," she said. "The pharaoh sends his greetings and wishes to express his thanks to the great king of Nubia. He speaks of the victory at hand for Egypt and seeks another favor of the king."

"I see," King Amani said, receiving the thick papyrus sheets from his sister and skimmed the message. "Princess Alodia, please call for the council members. We will meet in one quarter of an hour." King Amani left his throne.

Kandake entered the council chambers. Servants bustled about the room covering the top of a table along the side wall with platters of meat and herbs, cheese, thick slices of bread slathered with butter, and pitchers of thinned juice and water—an indication that this would be a long meeting. Thick hides covered with drawings of the boundaries of the surrounding kingdoms shrouded the bricks of the red-brown mud that made up the tall walls of the room. The maps served a two-fold purpose: they were an easy reference of the boundaries of the nearby kingdoms and they damped the words spoken within the room.

The council was made up of the king's siblings, two brothers and one sister. Alongside them sat the king's children who would take their positions on the council when it became Kandake's time to rule Nubia. The table, around which they sat, held a stone inlay of the kingdom of Nubia charting its hills and valleys, and where it reached the Nile River. Kandake took her seat at the head of the table next to her father, as the heir to his throne.

"The pharaoh has sent good news to Nubia," Aunt Alodia said, a crease forming between her brows.

Kandake paid careful attention to the words coming from her aunt. She had learned that the crease meant that there was something of concern for the kingdom.

"He is reporting that the war, started by Assyria, is almost at an end, leaving Egypt victorious. He states that this is due in large part to the accuracy of the Nubian bow and strength of our warriors."

Kandake made note of the faces of the council members. The expression worn by her uncle, Prince Naqa, Protector of Nubia's Wealth, was the easiest to read. The lines of worry were relaxing into gentle eddies of pleasure. She could almost see him counting the rings of gold that would be added to Nubia's treasury as promised by the pharaoh. Sitting next to him, her sister, Princess Tabiry, wore a nearly identical expression as she scratched notes on sheets of papyrus.

She has not yet learned to calculate the sums in her mind as Uncle has. Kandake felt the corners of her mouth tug into a small grin. She wasted no time erasing it. *She will learn before long.*

"The difficult part of the message is," her aunt continued, "five of our warriors have died in battle." She read their names.

The face of Uncle Dakká, Prime Warrior of Nubia, turned to stone. Kandake knew that one of the men who died was her uncle's dear friend, and as she watched, the harsh edges of sorrow carved themselves into the face of Prince Natasen. She had never known her brother to hide his losses well.

When it is his time to serve Nubia as Prime Warrior it will be very difficult for him when it becomes his turn to send men into battle. Her heart felt the weight of the loss for the warriors' families.

4

"Egypt will honor each of their families with a breeding cow as promised and an additional two rings of gold."

"Thank you, Princess Alodia," King Amani said. "Please be sure to give each of those families a breeding cow from my herds as well."

The king's face evidenced his deep sorrow. Kandake tallied the loss for those families. Some children had lost their mothers, others had lost their fathers, and she knew of two marriage ceremonies that would not be taking place. War was a painful thing for citizens of every kingdom.

"There is another item for the council to discuss," King Amani announced. "The pharaoh has asked for a contingent of warriors to remain in Egypt. He would like them to maintain order along the border where destruction and confusion is most prevalent."

Uncle Dakká's features hardened. Uncle Naqa's looked expectant. Kandake knew he was counting the rings of gold he would add to Nubia's treasury.

"The pharaoh states that several of our warriors have volunteered for this duty." King Amani poured himself a bowl of water. "I am not certain that this is so. We need to speak with our warriors to ensure these are their words and that their families are well cared for."

"My King," Alara, Kandake's oldest brother, said. "Do you believe the pharaoh to be misrepresenting the situation?" Alara sat next to Aunt Alodia. He would be advisor to Kandake when she ruled the kingdom as their aunt did for the king.

"No, I do not. But it is necessary that our warriors be provided the opportunity to speak for themselves and be heard by their kingdom."

2

"I will dispatch a warrior to speak with them, My King," Uncle Dakká said. "You will have your answer within a few days."

"Thank you, Prince Dakká," King Amani said. "But a warrior would not be able to reach the pharaoh of Egypt. I need someone who can discuss his concerns and learn of his true needs."

"Then I will send Prince Natasen. He would understand the warriors' concerns and be able to meet with Nakhtnebef and assess his needs."

King Amani nodded his approval. Natasen sat straighter in his chair. Kandake saw pride shine from her brother's eyes.

"Might I suggest Prince Alara go as well," Princess Alodia said. "It would give him firsthand experience of the perspective of another ruler. This would prove very useful as he advises Princess Kandake when it is her time to rule Nubia.

"Prince Naqa, once again, the kingdom has need for you to determine the value of a Nubian bow." King Amani's eyes met and held those of his older brother. "I am not certain of the danger this new duty will entail, but I do not believe that it will hold much less peril than fighting on the battlefield. Please discuss these matters with Prince Dakká and conclude a price that is appropriate."

Kandake accepted the bowl of pomegranate juice that a servant placed before her. As she sipped it she noted the gleam in her uncle's eyes as he scratched notes on sheets of papyrus. *I know that look. Uncle is going to be sure the pharaoh pays a good price.* Her sister, Tabiry, jotted her own notes and pushed them to their uncle for his approval. *She must have suggested something important to Uncle. Whatever it is, he has added it to his notes.*

"Princess Kandake." King Amani's voice snagged her attention. "This is a venture that requires your attention as well. It would be wise for you to observe our dealings with our neighbor. While you are in Egypt, take the time to get to know Khabebesh, Nakhtnebef's son that will rule after him. It will afford you insight into what you can expect from that kingdom during your rule."

"Yes, My King." Kandake set the bowl of juice aside. "Do you believe Egypt will need our warriors for long? I am not sure it is a good thing for them to be away from their families, nor should Egypt depend on this kingdom's support overly much."

"That is the reason I am sending Prince Natasen. His duty is to assess the situation and determine the extent of our neighbor's need. Egypt must have the power to stand on its own. Nubia cannot protect and provide for two kingdoms."

"That is true, My King," Uncle Dakká said. "The might of Nubia must remain within its own borders, wherever that may be."

Kandake caught a look shared between King Amani and Prince Dakká. The brothers often appeared to communicate without a word being said.

"Thank you, good servants," her uncle said, maintaining eye contact with the king. "Your service has been sufficient. The council can continue on its own." At that signal the servants and scribes left the room. Uncle Dakká secured the doors after the last one had left.

"What I am about to discuss must not be written," King Amani said. He took the time to meet the gaze of each member of the council with his own. He waited until everyone had set down their quill before he continued. "There is more going on in Egypt. The message contained a glyph from Nakhtnebef's own hand—a sign of danger. This combined with his request for Nubian warriors to remain within the kingdom is an indication that things are not well.

"There have been rumors that his advisor seeks power and that Nakhtnebef himself is losing strength. His illness is also under suspicion."

"Cannot Khabebesh rule in his place?" Alara asked.

"The pharaoh's advisor, Herihor, has convinced the people that Khabebesh yet lacks the wisdom to rule the kingdom and would require his assistance," Aunt

Alodia said. "He has even swayed Khabebesh to believe the same."

"It seems to me that the pharaoh of Egypt is clear in his request," Tabiry said. "If our warriors assist Egypt in restoring order, does it not solve the problem? And it increases the wealth of Nubia to do so." Tabiry looked down at the papyrus sheet that lay before her.

"It is true, Princess Tabiry, that our warriors will help maintain order, but I believe the pharaoh has something else in mind." Aunt Alodia looked to the king for permission to continue. At his nod, she unfurled the sheets that had come from Egypt.

"It is not what is said in the message, but more the way it is worded. That, coupled with the pharaoh's glyph next to his seal, intimates he fears an uprising within the kingdom."

"I still do not see that this is a problem for Nubia." Tabiry's voice took on the tone of one who refuses to see beyond what serves her.

"Princess Tabiry," Kandake said. "What Princess Alodia is trying to say is that if there is to be an uprising within Egypt, the fears of its citizens would cause our warriors to be viewed as enemies by everyone within that kingdom. They could also be used by either side or held hostage giving that faction power to obligate Nubia to aid them as ransom. If Nubia must fight, it would be better for this kingdom to rule all of Egypt."

"Rule Egypt?" Tabiry asked. "Are we planning to go to war with our neighbor?" Tabiry was incredulous. The accusation in her eyes stabbed at Kandake. "I thought you had learned your lesson with Aksum. War can only hurt Nubia. There is nothing in it to be gained from conflict with Egypt."

"Princess Tabiry," Uncle Naqa said, trying to calm her. "No one here has said we are planning to go to war. Princesses Alodia and Kandake are merely stating the situation."

"Do not tell me she has deceived you!" Tabiry straightened her back as if making herself taller would add force to her argument. "It has been but a few days since the trouble with Aksum. Surely you remember that it was her actions that nearly brought the two kingdoms to war; all because of a misunderstanding between Princess Kandake and the Prince of Aksum. I still do not understand why she would refuse to take him as her husband."

"Princess Tabiry, you know that the situation between Nubia and Aksum was not of Princess Kandake's making. You also know the danger to Nubia had she considered marriage with that prince." Uncle Dakká gripped the drinking bowl in front of him. The way his skin stretched across his knuckles made clear to all at the table that he was working to contain his anger.

"But if Princess Kandake had only—"

"That is enough!" King Amani said. "If you continue to think as a child, allowing your wishes and fears to guide you, Great Mother was mistaken in believing you to be capable of safeguarding and developing the wealth of this kingdom."

Tabiry grasped the pages before her and opened her mouth to speak.

"You are correct in assuming there is revenue to be earned if our warriors serve Egypt a bit longer, but there is more to consider than cattle and gold." Uncle Naqa laid a calming hand on Tabiry's arm. "We must always weigh the cost to this kingdom."

Kandake's eyes shifted from her father to her sister and then back to her father again. *How can she not see that this is about more than a few rings of gold? There are not enough cows to replace a life. Nor should we risk the stability of Nubia over this. And what has any of this to do with Aksum or Prince Gadarat!*

3

"Prince Gadarat is a young fool," King Amani said. "Let us hope Zoskales lives long enough for his whelp to gain wisdom before it is his time to rule that kingdom."

Tabiry's gaze was again upon Kandake, piercing and fierce. Kandake met her sister's scrutiny with her own. *Why does my sister blame me for everything that displeases her? The journey to Egypt will bring welcome reprieve from her moods.*

"Princess Tabiry has said aloud what is in my thoughts." King Amani shifted in his chair. The movement appeared to shed the annoyance he displayed toward his daughter. "Nubia cannot afford to be caught up in a civil war should the disturbance in Egypt come to that. This is the reason you are going there. I must know the truth." He took time to meet the gaze of Natasen, Alara, and Kandake, in turn.

"Each of you must ferret out the truth. Has the pharaoh's illness been caused by his advisor or someone under his control? Could Khabebesh rule Egypt, should things come to that? Would our warriors be employed to keep the piece or avert an attempt by the advisor to usurp Egypt's throne?

"These are questions you must find the answers to. Nubia must have this information before it commits to anything." King Amani turned all of his attention upon Tabiry. She maintained an expression that told everyone she would not be easily swayed.

"If Egypt is to be weakened from within it is better that Nubia rule that land. It is not in our best interest to allow one of our mutual enemies to take it. It would not be long before they look to our borders."

King Amani held up his had to forestall Tabiry's comments. "Look to your history. This would not be the first time Nubia has ruled that kingdom."

Kandake sat on the sill of the window of her rooms. From there she could look beyond the palace courtyard. Her view took in the many sights and sounds of the kingdom she loved: the laughter of children playing; the sight of women working together, dying cloth to be traded; the aroma of healthy cattle droppings. Kandake loved Nubia.

Father is right. To keep Nubia strong our neighbors must be at peace. Nubia cannot afford Egypt to be destroyed from within or have its borders overrun.

"What kind of friend are you?" Tabiry said coming up behind Kandake. "You sit gazing out of the window while Nubia is under threat of war."

"What are you complaining about, now?" Kandake said, her own peaceful respite disrupted. "There is no threat to Nubia. Father is only gathering information, trying to keep the threat away from this kingdom."

"Pretend if you like, but you heard Father. He contemplates war and you are agreeing with him." She placed her hands on her hips. "What will happen to your friend? Her marriage is only weeks old. If Nubia goes to war there will be no children from that marriage—not with Ezena out there on the battlefield." At this last, she wagged her finger in Kandake's face.

Kandake sucked in a deep breath and let it out at a deliberate, slow pace and released the tension from her muscles. A technique she had learned in her warrior training, it helped to calm her mind before she responded to her sister.

"Tabiry, I have no doubt Father has the wisdom to choose what is right for Nubia, whether I agree with him or not. At least he waits until he has gathered the needed information before he makes a decision for this kingdom." The look she gave her sister was challenging enough to cause Tabiry to shift her gaze.

"It is not that I question our Father's wisdom or his love for this kingdom." Tabiry fumbled with the folds of her skirts. "It is that if Nubia should go to war, how will Ezena have the time or opportunity to enjoy her marriage or build a family?"

Kandake searched her sister's face. Her refusal to meet Kandake's eyes, along with her fidgeting was more than enough for Kandake to realize there was something else on Tabiry's mind.

"Maybe it would put you at ease if you told me what is truly troubling you." Kandake laid a hand on her sister's shoulder.

Tabiry shook it off. "You know what is 'troubling' me! How can I choose a family if you insist on this kingdom going to war? Whether it is with Aksum or Egypt the outcome will be the same!" Tabiry stormed from Kandake's rooms.

Kandake raised her face toward the heavens. "Of all of the sisters that you have created, why did you give me this one."

4

Kandake left her rooms and went in search of Alara. Conversations with him always seemed to lead her in the proper direction. His manner was easy and he had a way of making her smile regardless of the concern. She found him in the company of several men, young and old.

Each member of the king's family wore an anklet of bronze bells. The circlet around Kandake's ankle was made of gold, marking her as the next to rule the kingdom. The rhythmic jingle alerted the gathering of her approach. The group rose in response to her arrival. Kandake nodded her head in recognition of their show of respect and waved them to their seats.

"Princess Kandake," the eldest member of the group said. "We were discussing the best breeding practices to insure strength of the herd. We would hear you thoughts."

"I am honored, great uncle, that you would hear from me," Kandake said, bowing in deference to the man's age. "But I have little knowledge of herds beyond feeding and maintaining their health." She sat down next to her brother, but positioned herself a short distance outside the circle of debate. At the end of the discussion, the siblings excused themselves and left the group.

"Do you ever wonder about the positions Great Mother appointed us to?" Kandake asked.

"After all that has happened, you cannot still doubt the wisdom of her choice for you to rule?" Alara brushed back the braids that blocked his view of his sister's face. "It has only been a few months since she Named you as our next ruler and already your skill has saved this kingdom. And not with your bow, alone!"

"I was thinking of our sister." They walked passed a group of young women working at grinding grain to flour. When her brother acknowledged them, they giggled and twittered among themselves. Kandake gave him a playful poke with her elbow.

"What about Tabiry?" Alara asked, ignoring his sister's jab. "She knows value and market almost as well as Uncle Naqa."

"I do not question her knowledge. It is her...her.... I am not sure what to call it." Kandake glanced over her shoulder at the young women. There was one whose gaze followed her brother. *Nedjeh's cousin, I must remember to ask Alara about her.*

"It is the way Tabiry meets life, which concerns me. She understands how to recognize the value of an item for trade without hesitation, but it is her discernment of people that troubles me."

"She has chosen Shen to become her husband. He is a good man and worthy of the position…unless there is something that you have not said." He stopped walking and stared at Kandake.

"No, no, Shen is fine. That is not what I am talking about." She urged her brother to keep walking. "It is the way she questions Father's decisions. Yet, it is not that she questions his wisdom. It is more that she fears the outcome of his decisions."

They came upon a band of children playing toss with a knot of colorful rags tied together. Within an instant Kandake and Alara were included in the game. Kandake pitched the knot high into the air, to the delight of young ones scampering and squealing to be the one to catch it. It landed on the ground near the smallest boy among the group. The cloth he wore tied about his hips was as colorful as the rags they played with. It was his turn to toss the ball of rags. He launched it with all his might, investing such effort that his feet left the ground raising a small cloud of dust. Even so, the tightly bound cluster of color barely cleared the top of Alara's head. Alara made a great show of straining to catch it.

On Alara's turn to pitch the rags, he pretended to stumble causing the orb to land within easy reach of the little one's grasp. He caught it. The look of surprise on his face was unmistakable, which was soon replaced with intense pride and pleasure. He bowed his appreciation to the prince. Alara returned the gesture.

Kandake watched them giggle together over their shared accomplishment. *It is clear he loves children. I wonder why Alara has never presented himself as a*

19

suitor to anyone in the kingdom. Does he never plan to marry?

They moved on from the game resuming their conversation.

"It is true that our sister allows her fears to drive her, but I am certain she will learn to leave this practice behind."

"I hope she does so, as well. The sooner she does, the better it will be for all of us." Kandake noticed they were coming near the palace. She slowed her steps, touching her brother's arm to do the same. "I worry that I will not have the patience to wait for her to do this on her own. Not long from now we will celebrate her marriage to Shen. He is a warrior and one day he will go into battle. Will she support his strength or poison him with her fear?"

"Now who is borrowing tomorrow's troubles?" He gave his sister a playful tug on the tiny golden bell that hung from one of her braids and strode into the palace.

Help me. Kandake pleaded to the listening gods. *I have a sister that fears the troubles that do not exist and a brother that ignores the ones that do.*

<u>5</u>

Kandake found her father studying a sheaf of papyrus sheets in the council chambers. The half-filled pitcher of water before him indicated he had been at it for some time. She slid into the seat across from him and waited until he acknowledged her presence.

"Thank you for coming," King Amani said. "It is very important that I speak with you before you go to Egypt." He poured himself a drink of water and one for her as well.

"Herihor is not to be trusted. We believe he is at the root of Nakhtnebef's illness. You must present yourself as strong. He must see the warrior within." King Amani leaned back in his chair. His eyes scrutinized every inch of his daughter. "You have made me proud. Great Mother chose what is best for this kingdom. Remember the lessons of Princess Alodia, but do not forget those of Prince Dakká. Herihor is a dangerous man. Do not hesitate to defend yourself."

"Yes, My King," Kandake said. "And the prince?"

"He presents as one without wisdom. I am not sure this is so. In Nubia a boy becomes a man long before his age. It is possible that Prince Khabebesh is only functioning within the space allowed him. If there is more to this young man it would harm no one for him to stretch his wings."

Kandake spent the remainder of the afternoon with her father in the council chambers listening to the instructions he had about Egypt and Pharaoh Nakhtnebef's rule. Much of what he said instructed his daughter in how to assess the nature of the Pharaoh's power, but here and there he would remind her of Herihor and his nefarious intent.

Kandake sat across a small table from Amhara. He had brought evening meal to be shared while Natasen and Kashta posted shield a short distance away. Of Kandake's four suitors, Amhara was the man she most admired. His being a warrior was not the only reason she preferred him. His even temper, his attention to detail when analyzing a situation or making plans, and his fierce loyalty to those he cared about; these were the things that she found most attractive.

"Shen is happy beyond measure since Princess Tabiry announced that he is to be her chosen." Amhara placed slices of meat and cheese onto a plate and passed it to the center of the table for Kandake to eat from. As one of Kandake's suitors he was careful to observe all of Nubia's customs, particularly that which stated he was not to touch her in any way. The two warriors standing nearby reinforced the obedience of this rule.

"I wish I could say the same for my sister." The change of expression on Amhara's face hurried Kandake's explanation. "She is so worried that something will disrupt or prevent her marriage ceremony that living with her is pure agony."

With his chuckle, the crease between his brows disappeared. He moved on to a different subject. "My herd is increasing," he said. "My cow delivered a healthy bull. His legs are sturdy and his appetite is strong. He suckles well and he appears to put on weight daily."

"She delivered a bull? That is wonderful."

"Yes, and in eight months or so he should be ready to mount. I can trade his service for a young cow—once we know the ride has been successful and the cow is with calf."

"I am very happy for you," she said. *Your skill as a warrior leaves no doubt of your ability to protect a family. I can also see your ability to provide for that family is certain. You are the man I'd hoped you were.* Kandake enjoyed the remaining time with Amhara.

She had other suitors, yet more and more Amhara was the one she would choose. But, as Great Mother had said, until the day she was ready to announce she would take a husband it was necessary that she spend time with all of her suitors. So Kandake arranged to spend time with each of them before she would leave for Egypt.

The next morning, Kandake prepared for an early morning walk with Nesiptah. He was the oldest of her suitors, but his calming spirit soothed her.

"It is good to see that you spend time with suitors other than your warrior," Tabiry said. "Maybe they can help you to see that there is more to life than the next battle."

Kandake turned to face her sister. "I am certain Great Mother named you to be the keeper of Nubia's wealth because of your understanding of trade and value, but that has little to do with how I choose my life or my husband."

"I am also the older sister." Tabiry placed one hand on her hip, she used the other hand to wag a finger at Kandake. "It is your duty to hear what I have to say."

"I will listen when you either have something new to say, or say something that is helpful." She pushed past Tabiry.

Kandake and Nesiptah exited the palace courtyard at a comfortable pace. Natasen and Kashta, posting shield, followed a short distance behind.

"I thought we would walk through the marketplace. There are some lengths of cloth that I wanted you to see," Nesiptah said. "The colors are so bright, they remind me of you."

As they walked in that direction, their conversation included the various places and people they passed along the way. It migrated from cattle to building, from building to children, from children to craftsmanship, and finally to the dyes used to make the vibrant colors of the cloth in the marketplace.

"I love the oranges and purples best," Kandake said. "They remind me of the Nubian sunset."

"Look at this one. The greens and reds have gold threads woven within the pattern. The way the thread dances throughout is like your laughter and determination." Nesiptah held the length of fabric out to Natasen. "Would you assist me please?" He turned to Kandake. "I am certain the pattern in this one would be well suited to the richness of your skin."

Natasen draped the cloth across Kandake's shoulders. Nesiptah was right. The reds and greens of the fabric were enhanced by the subtle gold threads that meandered throughout the pattern. Together they enriched the deep brown of her skin.

"It would please me to purchase this for you," Nesiptah said.

Kandake enjoyed the soft shimmer of the gold thread. She knew the colors were perfect for her. To have this fabric wrapped about her hips in a skirt would be ideal. There was one problem. The person she wanted to see her in it was not the man gifting it.

_6_

That afternoon Kandake made her way to her grandmother's rooms. Great Mother was in the middle of a discussion with Makeda, Kandake's best friend's grandmother. Kandake stood outside the door waiting to be invited in. She observed the two women laughing and sharing stories. She could not remember a time when her grandmother looked so young. It reminded her of her friendship with Ezena. A pang of loneliness struck her heart.

It had been days since she had spoken to her friend. It would be weeks longer because Ezena had taken a husband and the two of them would be closeted away in their wedding pavilion learning and developing the bond they would share for life.

"Please, come in, granddaughter." Great Mother's words broke into Kandake's thoughts.

Kandake took a few steps into the room and kneeled before her grandmother in a show of respect.

Great Mother patted the large pillow next to her, inviting Kandake to sit with the two women.

"Princess Kandake," Ezena's grandmother said. "It is good to see you again. You did well at my granddaughter's marriage ceremony. Her braids were tight and straight, you fed her well on her journey, and I could not miss the amulet of friendship with the throne you tied into her hair."

Kandake nodded her acknowledgement of the older woman's praise as she sat down. Great Mother passed her the dish of brined olives. She took two and popped one of them into her mouth.

"Makeda was a little disappointed that Ezena had chosen you to braid her hair. She was hoping the opportunity would be hers."

"Pay no attention to your grandmother," Ezena's grandmother said. "Zaria knows my fingers are in no condition to plait the fine and delicate rows into the beautiful design you created." She held out her hands for Kandake to examine. There was slight swelling around the joints, but Kandake had no doubt these strong hands were still nimble enough to have done the job.

"The problem was not her fingers," Great Mother said. "Makeda was too busy examining the cattle given them by Nateka's father and the fabric of the pavilion to have the time to braid your friend's hair."

Ezena's grandmother glared and gasped in shock at Great Mother's words, but her laughter followed too soon afterward for there to be any weight to her original response. Great Mother's laughter joined in. Kandake was sure the grin on her own face was stretched wide as she watched the antics of these old friends. She nibbled on the refreshments around her. Her favorites, brined olives, fresh radishes, and pomegranate juice were in great supply.

"Princess Kandake," Ezena's grandmother began through mirthful tears. "Is it true that Prince Gadarat is not allowed within Nubia without your express permission?"

"Makeda!" Great Mother said. "You cannot ask such a question. Rumors and wars are begun over much less!"

"Zaria, calm yourself. Everyone knows that the prince is filled with thoughts of himself; his own beauty and greatness. It was only a matter of time before a young woman had the strength and wisdom to see him for what he is. In Aksum his position overshadows who he is. Our young women only see what they will gain from a union with him.

"I am not asking to carry tales or cause unpleasantness between our kingdoms. I only want to be able to answer with the truth. I am certain I will be asked when I return to Aksum.

Kandake lowered her eyes. She ran her tongue over and around the olive pit in her mouth, wondering how she should answer. Every thought about Prince Gadarat saturated her mind with feelings of wrath and revulsion toward that deceitful and unprincipled man. Yet, to tell the truth about the contempt she felt for the prince would be offensive to the woman before her. Still, her mind would not allow any other response.

"Grandmother Makeda, how would you prefer I answer your question? Should I respond as the next queen of Nubia or as a dear friend to your granddaughter?"

"I would hear the truth," she said.

"Then I will do my best to answer you as both." She filled her lungs and as she expelled the long slow breath, Kandake brought her emotions under control. "Prince Gadarat is not one who understands, nor does he respect, the strength of the women of Nubia. His father, King Zoskales, has decided that it would be best for his son to learn more of Nubian culture before he returns."

"I believed it was something such as this. Prince Gadarat has not grown to the point of wisdom that ruling a kingdom requires. My household prays for long life for his father. It is our hope that this will give Prince Gadarat time to develop understanding and maturity."

"As do we," Great Mother said. "Nubia must have strong alliances with its neighbors." She straightened her skirts and rearranged the double strand of beads at her neck and changed the subject. "Grandchild, tell us about your suitors."

Kandake was glad for the change. The eagerness in the eyes of Ezena's grandmother said the same.

Where should she start? Images of the four men shifted through her mind, Semna, Irike, Nesiptah, and Amhara. Amhara always lingered in her thoughts—the deep rich color of his skin, the way his muscles rippled as he moved through the various warrior holds and stances, and his smile…forever bright and welcoming. Although he was pleasant to look upon, these were not the reasons she longed for his company. It was the man Amhara was. His honesty, willingness to work, loyalty to his friends, and easy manner, these were the things that kept him within Kandake's heart and mind.

7

"I have only four suitors," Kandake explained and named them. A look of pride shone from the face of Ezena's grandmother as Amhara's name was spoken.

"It pleases me that you have selected my grandson," Great Mother's friend said. "His mother had hoped Amhara would return to Aksum and choose his wife. I must confess that I had hoped he would do so as well. But Amhara is quite taken with you and our kingdom no longer holds any promise for him."

"Makeda!" Great Mother snatched at her friend's skirts. "Hold your tongue! Princess Kandake must not be influenced in any way. It is vital that her choice of husband be her own."

"I am not trying to guide your granddaughter in her choice. I was only—"

"Yes, you were only being a grandmother—a grandmother who wants her grandchild to be happy. In this instance it is necessary to look beyond what would please two grandmothers. We must look to what is best for an entire kingdom."

Kandake listened to the debate between the old friends about what would constitute a good choice of husband for a queen. She had understood the importance of not being influenced in her choice so that all would know the voice of her rule was truly hers. Kandake also understood the necessity of choosing someone that would respect her rule. *But I must also decide what is best for me and not just Nubia's throne. How do I know what that is?*

Her mind sifted through the men that she had accepted as suitors. She had only selected four from among the many that had presented themselves. Kandake reexamined their qualities and attributes in light of how they would affect the kingdom. *Semna is a talented artisan and most generous. I am certain this would help to preserve our culture and all things of Nubia. Irike is a hard worker and his laughter comes with ease. In difficult times he would lighten my heart and never shirk what duties come to him. Nesiptah's ways would be soothing at the end of the day and he manages disputes with gentleness. Then there is Amhara.* Kandake felt the muscles of her cheeks shift as the smile in her heart slipped over her face.

He is a strong warrior. Honor abides within him. His loyalty is without question and he is able to determine patterns and flaws within people and plans. It was clear to Kandake that a marriage to any one of these men would be good for the kingdom, but her preference always came back to Amhara. Yet, should he be her choice? In Nesiptah's presence she felt at total ease and encouraged.

"Your pardon, Great Mother," she said, breaking into her grandmother's conversation. The two women focused their attention on Kandake. "If I am to choose a husband, a man I would spend my life with, do I concentrate on what is best for the kingdom, alone? Or, do I choose according to what is the better fit for me?"

The friends began another debate on how best to answer her question. Each told Kandake, at length, how they thought she should make her choice. Her grandmother spoke of the importance of choosing a husband for the good of the kingdom. Her grandmother's friend made the point of the importance of choosing a husband that was not only a good fit, but also the man's understanding of her heart. Kandake listened to them both, paying close attention to the points each made.

First, she looked to her grandmother. Her passion of what was right for Nubia did not falter. *Great Mother argues with certainty about what she believes is best for Nubia.* Then Kandake examined the face of Ezena's grandmother. *She is equally as certain. How could they both be so certain about what I should do and their solutions so different?*

The more Kandake listened, the more confused she felt. *It is as if my mind and heart are battling against each other.*

She listened to the arguments made by the older women again; trying to determine which one fit her best. The more she listened, the more unsettled she became. Her mind pulled her one direction and her heart wrenched her in another. Kandake employed a warrior exercise to relieve her mounting tension, but to no effect.

She sent her mind through the exercise again, but still found no ease. The voices of the women debating back and forth added to her discomfort. At last, Kandake could no longer tolerate the mounting conflict within.

"Your pardon, please," Kandake said as she stood. She left the women to their discussion and went in search of the one thing she knew would calm her.

8

Kandake walked into the center of the training floor in the warrior compound. Her gaze traveled about the room trying to determine which exercise would help her battle through the war within. Frames holding man-shaped, straw-filled figures taunted her from the corners of the room, but they did not quite offer what she was looking for.

Against the wall, piles of more of the same forms lay waiting for her to abuse them in whatever brawl she could imagine. Yet, these held no appeal for her. Kandake meandered over to the wall from which multiple types of shields hung. She lifted one from its hook and hefted its weight. It felt good to her.

Sliding the holds into place, Kandake danced about the training floor in mock battle, blocking knife thrusts and spear tosses.

What has come over me? I may not be certain of the man I should choose, but I am certain of who I am!

It is not necessary to change who I am to choose a husband nor will choosing a husband change who I am!

She worked up a light sheen of perspiration and looked for more to add to this dance. Kandake walked across the training surface to the container that held a cache of long-knives. It was a closely-woven basket of grasses reinforced with strands of wire. She tested several knives for length and balance until she found one that suited her, then she began her practice in earnest.

I may become the queen, but I will always be a warrior! I am Princess Kandake warrior and future queen of the kingdom of Nubia!

Kandake held her shield before her as if in defense. She kept her long-knife at the ready as if awaiting an opening from her opponent. She thrust her blade forward then swept it upward parrying the imagined overhead strike.

Her next move had her using the shield to strike the side of her adversary's head and brought her blade across in follow through with a downward blow between neck and shoulder. Pulling her blade free from her imaginary enemy, she employed a back-swing of the weapon with a backward pivot to face the enemy at her rear.

This is who I am. This is what I do!

"Uncle, your pardon, please," Kandake said, as she stopped the blade just short of slicing a great gash into his neck.

"No pardon needed," Uncle Dakká said. "Your footwork is not even. Work the revolution again. The placement of your blade is accurate, but your turn does not have balance."

Kandake worked through the move again.

"That was better. Try it once more at a slower pace, then you will feel where to place your weight."

"I can feel the difference," she said, working at the turn several more times.

"Now, Princess, come at me." Uncle Dakká stood before her armed as she was with long-knife and shield.

Kandake advanced and swung her blade. Uncle Dakká knocked it away using his shield and thrust his knife toward her. Kandake parried his attack using the flat side of her weapon. This allowed her to use a backswing and spin into him.

He blocked her strike, slid the edge of his blade down the length of hers bringing the weapons hilt to hilt. Iron rang against iron, singing out into the room. Kandake used her shield to clout the side of her uncle's head.

Uncle Dakká turned with the blow reducing its sting and brought himself back into position to strike, knocking Kandake from her feet. She hit the floor with an audible slap.

"Your skill and strength are growing, Princess." Uncle Dakká extended a hand to assist Kandake from the floor. "Upon your return from Egypt you will find that your training schedule will include more time with the long-knife." He took the blade from her and returned it, along with his, to the standing basket. He directed her to rehang their shields.

"Princess, may I see the blade you wear?"

Kandake pulled the knife that she wore at her hip from its sheath and extended it to her uncle.

"I am speaking of the gift from Natasen."

Kandake reached inside her skirt just below the waistband and removed the small dagger. Her brother had crafted the knife. He hardened the blade by hammer insuring that it would hold its edge. The tang ran through the hilt to the length of the handle giving it strength and balance. Natasen had given it to Kandake just before she left to rescue Alara.

Uncle Dakká flipped the small knife through the air several times catching it by handle or tip, without err. "Its balance is good." He ran his thumb along its slender edge and then drew it across the length of his arm, shaving off the fine hairs. Kandake had seen Natasen do this many times. He returned the dagger. "Good, you keep a keen edge. Now let me see you use it."

9

At the end of a much longer session than she had intended Kandake returned to her rooms. It was time for evening meal. Although it had become her practice to share it with Ezena, her friend's recent marriage changed this. Kandake now developed the habit of eating the meal in her rooms using the time to be alone with her thoughts.

She took the time to wipe her arms, neck, and face with a dampened piece of softened hide. *The hard work with Uncle was good. I feel more like myself.* She walked over to the table where servants had left evening meal for her and selected several slices of roasted meat and strong cheese for her plate. It pleased her to see a small bowl of brined olives. There was also a plate of radishes and onions.

Kandake took the filled plate to the chair nearest one of the tall windows and sat looking out upon Nubia.

I expected that becoming the next ruler of the kingdom would require much of me. I am willing to be everything Nubia needs.

Kandake lifted a slice of roasted meat to her mouth and savored a generous bite. She sucked its juices from her fingers and giggled at the mental image of her sister's disapproving glare. She followed this with a piece of onion and a morsel of strong cheese. The flavors on her tongue melded into something pleasant. She washed it down with a swallow of her favorite drink, pomegranate juice.

I never thought I would want to marry, but now I find myself receiving suitors and enjoying it. My thought at the time was to accept Amhara and no one else. Great Mother insisted that I receive others unless I was ready to make him my husband. Amhara as my husband.... The muscles of her face pulled. She felt the smile as it blossomed. *It is a pleasant thought, but I am not ready for marriage.*

She took another bite of cheese and followed that with a brined olive. A scene outside her window caught her attention. A small girl chased a baby goat. Every time she caught up with it she would attempt to bundle it in her arms. The problem was that she was not much larger than the goat. Her grasp only encompassed the animal's head, neck and shoulders. This left its hind legs free to drag in the dust of the ground. The trailing hooves raised a cloud around them that startled the small beast causing it to buck and freeing itself would only to begin the chase again.

Kandake smiled at the sight. *Having a child would be pleasurable and satisfying.*

She drank more of her juice and thought of her future and children as she continued watching the events unfolding before her. The faces of her suitors Semna, Irike, Amhara, and Nesiptah flowed through her mind as she tried to imagine having children with each of these men. It was no surprise to her that she could not envision children with Semna or Irike. Nor was there any great wonder that she could imagine them with Amhara. Yet it amazed her that she could imagine having children with Nesiptah.

Kandake recollected the days and meals that she had shared with him. *He is pleasant to be with. And his company is restful.*

The mother of the small child she had been watching came and scooped the girl up in her arms, then tied her to her back with a wide cloth. Once the child was settled and secure, the woman lifted the young goat and went about her business.

She compared the two men. The qualities of Nesiptah were relaxing and peaceful. She found him easy to talk to. *He is much like Alara in that way.*

Amhara is more like me. He understands my need to protect this kingdom. Honor and loyalty are very strong within him. Kandake brought a clear image of Amhara's smiling face to mind. The muscles in her face returned that smile automatically. *It is very clear to me that my feelings for Amhara are strong, but my care for Nesiptah grows within me.*

This was a discussion she would have taken to Ezena, but she was not available. Kandake pondered going to her grandmother. *Her thoughts are of what is best for the kingdom, but I must also choose what is best for me.*

She considered asking her mother. *Her heart leads her and her children are most important. There are times when Nubia must be my first consideration.*

Kandake sat thinking of the women she most respected as she gazed at the land from her window. The person she needed to discuss this with had to be someone that loved Nubia as much as she did. It must be someone who understood the needs of the kingdom and yet appreciated the importance of family. And above that, it must be a person that grasped the power and position of a ruler.

<u>10</u>

Kandake stood outside the door to her aunt's residence. The house was within a short walk of the palace. It had been built at the top of a knoll and was positioned to catch the breeze that blew across the Nile River. She raised her hand to knock on the door, but a servant opened it before her hand struck the wood.

"Good evening, Princess Kandake," the servant said. "A message has been taken to Princess Alodia of your arrival."

Kandake stepped inside, accepting the bowl of cool water extended to her. The large room had a low table at its center. Scattered across its top were dishes containing the remnants of the evening meal that had be recently eaten there. In the corners of the room stood tall lampstands with lit bowls of oil whose flames flickered shadows on the walls behind them.

The air smelled of incense burning to mask the odor of the meal that had been prepared within the home.

"Princess Kandake!" Aunt Alodia said. Her voice was warm, rich, and full of the pleasure that appeared on her face at seeing her niece. "Come sit with me while I put Kheb to bed."

Kheb, Aunt Alodia's youngest child, was almost eight years old and more than old enough to put herself to bed, but it was a practice that pleased them both.

Kandake found Kheb resting on her bed.

"Cousin," Kheb shouted. She clambered to her knees. "There is talk that you will go to Egypt and bring our warriors home."

Kandake turned toward Aunt Alodia.

"Mother never tells me anything. I have to go skulking around the kitchens to learn what happens in this kingdom." She moved to the edge of her bed and patted it for Kandake to sit next to her. "I would go with you but I know they will not let me." She glared at her mother. "Uncle will not even allow me to train in the compound. He says that I am too young. That is not true, I am nearly as old as you were when you began to train."

Words poured from Kheb's mouth. Neither Kandake nor Kheb's mother could get a word in. "I have made a sling and I practice with it every day. Mother, Father and Uncle say that I am too small to draw a bow, so I use my sling, and I run. I run to the Nile and then through the fields. I will be fast and my sling will be accurate. I desire to become a warrior just like you."

"That may be," her mother said. "But for now, you will lie on your bed and sleep until morning."

"Yes, Mother," Kheb said, through a wide-mouthed yawn. "Cousin, you will say good-bye before you leave for Egypt, please?" This last she said with eyes closed and her voice thick with sleep.

Kandake walked with her aunt to a small courtyard on the side of the house. Once they were settled, servants brought them bowls of cool water and slices of honeyed figs.

"It has been some time since you and I have had an opportunity to visit," her aunt said. "Tell me how are you adjusting to the changes in your life?"

"Some of them are more difficult to live with than others," Kandake said.

"At least you no longer have the burden of Prince Gadarat as a suitor."

"I do not." Kandake sipped from her bowl and set it on the small table next to her. She took one of the sweet treats and picked at it. *I had no desire to have him as a suitor and much less as a husband.*

"My niece, your face is knotted like the tangled briars of the field. What is troubling you?"

"Auntie, I am not yet ready to choose a husband."

"No one says you must."

"Not long ago I would have told you that Amhara would be my choice, but now…." She set the fig back on the plate and scrubbed at her hands with a clean piece of linen.

"Has Amhara done something to change how you feel about him?" Her voice was low and calm, but the alertness of her eyes was a clear indication that she was prepared to protect her niece from all harm.

"He has done nothing, Auntie, except be the man he has always been." Kandake set the cloth aside. "I only ever wanted one suitor, but now I have four. Irike and Semna will never be anything more than what they are right now." She cast her gaze to the floor, not certain how to explain her problem. Aunt Alodia waited for her to continue.

"I need wisdom. I do not know how to choose. Great Mother says that I must choose a husband that will be best for Nubia. Mother says that I must choose a husband that is best for me. Which is it, should I choose as Great Mother says, or my mother? How do I know who is right?" Kandake clenched her fists in her lap.

Aunt Alodia laid her hand upon her niece's arm. "I would say they have both given you the wisdom you seek." When Kandake opened her mouth to speak, her aunt gave her arm a gentle squeeze. "You must choose a husband that is both of these things—a husband that is good for you and good for Nubia."

11

A few days later Kandake had packed and was ready to leave for Egypt. She tied her remaining bundle behind the saddle on Strong Shadow's back. The party consisted of Kandake, Alara, Natasen, and Shen. She returned to her rooms for the last of her things.

Kandake picked up a bag of sling stones and tied it about her waist, adjusted the fastenings of her breastplate, and slipped her bow over her head. As she settled it into place across her body, Tabiry stepped through the doorway.

"It would appear from the way you are dressed that you have forgotten Father's instructions," Tabiry said. "You are not there to start a war, but to gather information."

"A warrior is always prepared for battle." Kandake slipped the strap of her quiver over her shoulder and readjusted the fall of her bow. "And before you say it, I am being cautious about the travel between Nubia and Egypt."

"We share a common border with Egypt. As we are not at war with them, I see no need for you to be dressed like that." The sweep of her hand included Kandake's breastplate, bow, knife, and sling.

"There are things you have not taken the time to consider, my sister. Egypt is just ending a war with the Assyrians and we still have not found the origin of the bandits that have attacked our caravans." Kandake blew out a breath of exasperation. She did not expect her sister to understand everything about battle, but if she was not always looking for something to criticize, life would be a lot more pleasant.

Satisfied that she had correctly placed her armor and weapons, Kandake left her rooms and walked toward the palace courtyard. She met her father at the bottom of the steps and bowed her respect.

"Princess Kandake," her father said, beckoning her to rise. "Within this pouch is the armband establishing your authority to speak for the throne of Nubia. I also had the healer to include a packet of herbs and medicines to assist Nakhtnebef with whatever illness he may have."

"Thank you, My King," Kandake said. She tied the pouch to a ring on her belt, kissed her mother good-bye, and vaulted to Strong Shadow's back. As the party rode beyond the warriors' compound on their way out of Nubia, Kandake caught sight of Amhara. Having his bow with them would have meant added security for their journey, but his presence would not have assisted in their objective—determining the truth of the power in Egypt. That could only be gleaned from conversations with Pharaoh Nakhtnebef or Prince Khabebesh and Amhara was not in a position to do either.

It would take them a little more than two days to reach the pharaoh's palace riding their horses as hard as they dared. Natasen and Shen took turns riding next to Kandake providing added protection for the next ruler of Nubia. As the sun began to lower in the sky, Natasen called a halt to the travel for the day leading them to a secure campsite.

"We will break the night into four watches. I will take the first and Shen with take the last. Kandake, that leaves you and Alara to take the second and third."

"Then I will begin preparing the evening meal," Alara said. "I brought dried meat, onions, and hard rolls."

"I saw a few wild radishes over there," Kandake said. "They would be a welcome addition to a stew."

Shen collected the makings for a cook fire while Kandake went to gather the vegetables she had seen. When the meal was prepared, Kandake took a bowl to Natasen where he stood watch.

"Do you see anything?" she asked, staring off into the savannah.

"No, I do not expect trouble as we are still within Nubia's borders." He accepted the food from his sister. Though he began eating, Natasen kept his gaze roving over the land.

"Then you believe we may be attacked the closer we get to Egypt?"

"There is always that possibility. Neither Uncle Dakká nor Father believes Herihor can be trusted. He knows that we are coming to speak with our warriors and perhaps the pharaoh as well." He dipped his bread into the broth of the stew and bit off the moistened area. "If he is as treacherous as they believe, then his best course of action is to make certain we do not arrive."

"Would he not worry that our father would retaliate against Egypt?"

"Not while he has Nubian warriors sworn to protect that kingdom."

Kandake leaned her shoulder against a nearby tree. Her mind was a jumble of thoughts and feelings. *Would Herihor use Nubian warriors against Nubia? Would they fight?* The answer made itself clear to her. There was no question about what would happen if Herihor was as dangerous a man as her father made him out to be. He would require Nubia's warriors to hold true to their pledge to serve the throne of Egypt. And yes, they would fight as a matter of honor.

Rage flooded her being. This man had to be stopped. It was her duty to Nubia, the kingdom she loved and the kingdom she would one day rule.

12

The next morning Kandake relieved Shen from his watch to get something to eat before they broke camp. Her gaze scoured the area ahead of them as far as she could see looking for possible dangers to her small group. The outlands of Nubia stretched before her—hard ground with patches of grass and dry brush. Yet, it was part of her home, a land she loved. Behind her were the sounds of blankets being shaken out and utensils being packed, horses being watered, and the sizzle of the fire being doused.

"Good morning, my sister, future queen of Nubia," Alara said, coming to stand next to Kandake. "How was your sleep?"

"I slept well, thank you." She turned to look at her brother. "You are making a point of my status and position. You only do this when conveying a message. What would that be, brother?"

"When you step into Egypt they must see you as you are and as you will be. You are the throne of Nubia with whom they will conduct all transactions, today and all of the tomorrows to come.

She locked her gaze with his. "And the warrior within?"

"The warrior must be every bit as present as the queen."

"The horses have been watered and saddled," Natasen said, interrupting. "It is time for us to leave."

Kandake and Alara walked to their horses and mounted. The cool of the morning and the rest from the night before made it possible for the horses to move at a steady gallop. This allowed them to cover a good bit of ground. Soon they would come upon what the Egyptians referred to as the 'red land', the barren desert. Here they would have to spare their horses as much as possible, walking if need be.

The changes in the landscape were subtle but definite as they traveled. They had left the lushness of Nubia behind, traveling through the outlands of the kingdom. Within a few measures they would be entering the barren desert of Egypt.

Natasen called for a rest for the horses. As Kandake dismounted, she removed one of the skins of water she carried. Tucked within her pack was a bowl-shaped skin designed for Strong Shadow; this she filled with water. Her horse needed no encouragement to drink. Once he was satisfied, Kandake wiped the inside of his nostrils with what remained. After Strong Shadow's needs were met she saw to her own, drinking her fill and removing her riding cape from her pack.

Kandake tied the heavy cloak about her shoulders and climbed into the saddle. She then spread the tail of the wrap over the beast's rump and pulled the hood over her head doing what she could to protect them both from as much of the sun as possible.

"Keep the horses at an easy walk," Natasen said.

The small party rode two abreast, keeping a vigilant watch on the terrain around them. They surveyed for dangers to their horses—sharp rocks or sudden holes; and dangers for themselves—bandits or agents of Herihor. They traveled at a slower pace, sparing their horses in the intense heat. The desert sun lowered in the sky creating streaks of purple and orange. At Natasen's signal the group dismounted, sparing their horses at the last part of the long day of travel.

"This is the time we need to be most watchful," Natasen said. His voice lowered so that it would not carry beyond those that traveled with him. "If Herihor means us harm, this is the time his agents would strike."

As if on cue, a sling-stone kicked up dust at Strong Shadow's fore hoof. The next one hit him on the leg, startling the horse and causing him to pull away from Kandake's grasp. Kandake, Natasen, and Alara dropped to the ground. Shen vaulted to his horses back and galloped after the frightened beast.

Sharp hand signals from Natasen directed Kandake to make quick work of hobbling the remaining horses. To be without a horse in this hostile territory would mean certain death to the travelers.

Stones continued to fly at their horses in an attempt to run them off.

"Can you see the direction the stones are coming from?" Alara asked.

"I am not certain, but I believe them to be directed from two locations. Natasen pointed toward a small mound in front of them and another to their left.

"Whoever is attacking is not aiming at us, only our mounts," Kandake said.

"I do not believe they are aiming much at all. Look at how their stones fall; only in the general direction of the horses." Natasen inched toward his sister.

Kandake watched as a volley of stones came over the mound to the left. "If I crawl back the way we came, I should be able to circle around behind them."

"That is a possibility, but we do not know their number."

"No, we do not. But I would rather fight them in the remaining sunlight than wait until darkness falls." Kandake slipped her bow from her back and held it in one had as she crawled away. Sliding along the ground forced sand inside her breastplate. Her body slickened from the day's heat caused the sand to stick to her skin. With every movement the grains rubbed and scraped at her flesh. It began as an annoyance and then developed into discomfort. It became painful just as Kandake had made her way behind their attackers.

The lowering sun only allowed enough light to see two shadowed figures crouching behind the mound.

Kandake nocked an arrow to her bow, took aim, and let fly. The shaft buried its head deep at the side of one man's neck. The figures spun to face her. The one on the left gathered his feet beneath him to launch an attack.

"My next arrow will bury itself in your neck." Kandake's voice was low and menacing.

The man on the right made a sharp movement with his arm. A knife sped through the air in her direction as the other man came at her. She loosed the arrow and it found its mark within the knife-thrower's neck. Before she could nock another, the surviving agent was upon her.

Kandake filled both fists with his garment and twisted as he slammed her to the ground. Continuous sessions within the warrior compound taught her to keep her legs on the outside. As his back crashed in the dirt, Kandake was on her knees straddling her opponent.

The feel of his body was strong, battle hardened. She knew her actions must be quick, his strength outmatched hers. He brought his hand up to circle her neck. Kandake leaned in with her forearm across his. She dug her toes into the dirt and added the strength of her legs to the force of her arm, cutting off his airway. She punched the side of his head in a rapid tattoo. After what felt like an eternity, the man lost consciousness.

Kandake rolled away from his body. With the grace of long practice, she climbed to her feet, pulling her knife from its sheath as she rose. The sound of hooves against sand alerted her to an attack at her back. She turned in a low crouch ready to spring upon its rider.

Shen dismounted as the horse cleared the top on the mound and came to stand next to her.

"Are you harmed, Princess Kandake?" he asked. His eyes swept over her.

"No, I am not injured." She panted from the exertion. Turning in the direction of the other mound of dirt, she said "There are more hiding over there."

"Princes Natasen and Alara have dealt with them. Their attackers have not survived." He looked toward the man with the arrow protruding from his neck and at the one lying at her feet. "This one lives?"

13

Shen examined the unconscious man. Kandake stood next to him. The man lying in the dirt was clothed in the robes of an Egyptian. His skin coloring was somewhat of a surprise. It was pale. She had expected the rich red-brown of the Egyptian people. The hair escaping from the cap hugging his head was the color of night and as straight as a pulled iron rod.

"I feel as if I should know this man," she whispered. "It is almost as if I have met him."

"I do not believe you know him, Princess. Nor do I." Shen's voice held an edge that she had not heard him use since the night he had captured Kandake and her friends trying to drive away their horses.

"What is it?" she asked. Natasen and Alara joined them.

"This man is from Scythia. I do not know what he is doing in this desert or why he is wearing clothing such as this."

Kandake looked back and forth between the man lying on the ground and the one standing next her. This attacker shared the same hue of skin a Shen, honey brown. Their eyes held the same tilt at the corners as they rode above widened cheeks. The biggest difference for her, the man standing next to her had earned her respect and friendship.

"The men we fought with were of Egypt," Alara said. "What of that one?" He pointed to the man bearing Kandake's arrow.

They walked the short distance. Natasen stretched him out for ease of inspection.

"Scythian!" Shen spat out a phrase that Kandake could not understand. The expression on Alara's face told her what he said was no compliment.

"Strip them," Natasen ordered. "We will bury the dead, but this one," he nodded in the direction of their unconscious attacker, "we will take to Egypt with us, along with their clothes and weapons."

Three of them wrangled the robes and weapons from the bodies of the dead while Natasen bound and stood guard over the other. Shen and Alara dug the graves leaving Kandake free to prepare evening meal.

There would be no cooking fire this night owing to the possibility of others lying in wait. Kandake divided up cold rations of dried beef, crisp onions, and dried dates and began attending to their horses. She had finished rubbing them down and was pouring water into their bowls when Alara and Shen joined her.

.

"I would know what that—," another word that Kandake did not know, "is doing in Egypt?" Shen spat on the ground.

"Many people come to Egypt from different parts of the world, just as you are in Nubia." Alara pulled a treat from a pouch tied about his waist and gave it to his horse.

Shen grumbled something unintelligible as he examined the hooves of his mount.

"Why does the presence of this man disturb you?" Kandake asked, coming to stand next to Shen.

"Do you not remember the killing of my Sovereign's representative? He came to this land to build alliances with the peoples here."

"I remember."

"Though I do not know him, this man has the look of a warrior. As one serving the Sovereign, it was his duty to die with the Emissary or return to Scythia with the ironstone token of the Sovereign. He did neither!" Shen released the hoof he was cleaning. He stepped away from the horse to glare at their prisoner.

"It is time for evening meal." Kandake laid a hand of encouragement upon his arm.

They walked toward the area designated as their camp for the evening. There Natasen carried an assembled portion of travel rations toward the bound man.

"What are you doing?" Shen barked.

"I am feeding him."

"He has not earned his meal. We have yet to question him." Shen stood between Natasen and the prisoner.

"The desert is a harsh place. He must eat to have strength to talk." Natasen moved to step around him.

Shen blocked his path and grasped the pouch of food. "Then water only. If you feed him, he will not have respect for the Nubian warrior."

Natasen made a sound of dismissal.

"It is our way, Friend." Shen locked his gaze with Natasen's.

Natasen stared at the bound Scythian, nodded at Shen and released the food pouch. He returned to sit with Kandake and Alara and ate his own meal. Shen followed.

"Will you not feed him?" Alara asked, nodding toward their captive.

"Scythian warriors eat before they feed their prisoners. If he eats before you, he thinks himself a guest." Shen bit off a piece of the dried meat. He made a show of savoring his meal. He sucked hard on the spout of the water skin, taking the liquid in great gulps. Natasen followed his example.

Their captive yelled a spate of words from his bound position. Shen responded with his own vitriolic phrase. Kandake looked to Alara to translate.

"He says we will be dead by morning, killed before we wake," Alara translated. "Shen told him that only dogs and traitors die in their sleep."

Kandake rose from her meal, snatched up her bow, and took the first watch. "Brother," she yelled from her position. "Please ask him which is better for a Scythian warrior, to die in his sleep or to be bested by a woman?" The snickers of Shen and Natasen reached her where she stood. Their snickers developed into howls of laughter as Alara translated her message.

_14_

The night passed without any further attacks upon the small party. Their captive was tied to a litter dragged behind Kandake's horse across the remaining distance to Egypt. As they rode into the palace courtyard, people gathered to witness the spectacle. Kandake dismounted and stood over their prisoner glaring as Natasen cut him loose.

Once freed, the Scythian jumped up from the litter and took a swing at Kandake. She ducked the blow, stepped forward at an angle, pivoted off her back foot and drove a punch from her shoulder into his middle. She used the forward motion to get behind him and connected a backswing to the base of his skull. The man went down as if filled with straw.

Kandake pounced on him with one knee on the ground and the other in the small of his back. Grabbing a fistful of his hair, she yanked his head backward and put her blade to his throat. Whispers circulated throughout the watching crowd. What she heard most often was the question, "Who is this woman that conquers men?"

She kept the Scythian in this hold until addressed by a member of the Egyptian guard. "This man is a citizen of Egypt and a member of Pharaoh's royal personal guard. How dare you threaten his life?" He reached to pull Kandake away.

"Since when does Egypt threaten the throne of Nubia?" Alara bellowed, stepping between the guard and his sister. "This one attacked the representative of King Amani of Nubia. You would be wise to grant us audience with Pharaoh Nakhtnebef before you add further insult to the alliance of our two kingdoms."

"And who is this representative of Nubia?" the guard said. He looked from Alara to Natasen and back to Alara, again.

"Princess Kandake, future queen and ruler of the kingdom of Nubia." Alara's voice carried to every corner of the courtyard.

At his announcement, Kandake gave control of their prisoner over to Shen who placed his foot where her knee had pinned the man to the ground. She sheathed her knife and came to stand before the Egyptian guard. Kandake's bearing, shoulders squared, chin erect, informed all present of her importance. Her withering gaze directed at the man standing before her sent him scurrying to report her arrival. The guard's obvious haste sent up another spate of whispers among the crowd.

Before long, the guard returned with the several servants, another of the Egyptian guard, this one with apparent ranking, and the last man to come out of the pharaoh's palace strutted like a peacock. He strode up to the small party from Nubia and stopped in front of Kandake.

"Am I to understand that Egypt has been graced with the presence of the next ruler of Nubia, Princess Kandake?" He reached for her hand.

Kandake took a step backwards allowing Alara and Natasen to stand between her and this man.

"Please forgive me," the man said. "I have not introduced myself. I am Herihor, Tjaty to Pharaoh Nakhtnebef, his advisor." He stood before them as if waiting for something.

Neither the knowledge of your name or position grants permission. A Nubian woman chooses those with whom she is intimate.

When neither Kandake, nor those with her, said anything Herihor continued.

"I understand that you have experienced some difficulty along your journey to Egypt. I also am told that you believe this man to be a part of that difficulty.

"It is more than a belief. He was caught during the attack," Natasen said. He crossed his arms over his chest and jutted out his chin as if challenging Herihor to dispute this statement.

"I find that difficult to believe. This man is a member of Pharaoh's royal personal guard—a man to be trusted." He turned to face Shen. "Yet, your man has his foot on him, holding him in the dirt, treating him like a slave."

"We cannot speak to his rank or position, only to the behavior he has displayed," Alara said.

"If you please," Herihor said. "Allow the man to rise and give an accounting of himself."

The ranking guard strode to Shen, stood in front of him with his hand resting on the sword he wore at his side as if to intimidate. Shen kept his eyes forward ignoring the maneuver. Given a hand signal from Natasen, Shen released the man.

Freed, the man climbed to his feet, brushed himself off and growled a Scythian oath under his breath to Shen. Through a wicked grin Shen responded something that caused the man to increase the distance between the two of them at a hurried pace and did not slow until he came to Herihor's side.

"These of Nubia suggest that you intended them harm," Herihor said. "I am certain there must be some misunderstanding." He turned to the man beside him.

Kandake stared at the advisor. *A smile moves across this Tjaty's face as the serpent moves across the sand of the desert. I can see the wisdom of Father not to trust you.*

"Tjaty," the man bowed low, "we meant no harm. We went to find them in the desert, as you instructed, to lead them to the palace. We tossed a few stones at their mounts. It was meant to be a harmless prank, frightening their horses."

"Frightening a traveler's horses in the desert is no prank, neither is it harmless!" Natasen's rage filled every word. "This one intended that we be stranded and die."

"Not so, Tjaty! Not so. It was a silly game, an ill-conceived trick. It was never our intent to harm them."

"And the knife your companion threw at me, that was not proposed as harm?" Kandake glared at the pharaoh's advisor waiting for the explanation.

"Facing a Nubian with a bow drawn, one must believe his life to be in jeopardy." He shrugged his shoulders as if this explained everything.

"Report to your captain!" Herihor dismissed the man. "He will be suitably punished, I assure you."

This interchange assured Kandake of one thing, if this man were punished it would be for not succeeding in stranding them in the desert.

"The servants will escort you to your rooms." Herihor said. "Please do not allow the behavior of a fool to spoil your visit to Egypt. I will inform Pharaoh Nakhtnebef of your arrival."

Of the group of servants, several of them collected their belongings from their horses. Those remaining led their horses away.

"And what of this man?" Herihor said, indicating Shen as he came to stand behind Kandake. "How shall we house your slave?"

"Shen is no one's slave. He is a free man," Alara said. "He protects Princess Kandake."

The small party of Nubians was taken to their rooms. Shen was shown to a room near Kandake. This he denied and requested a mat. He laid it across her doorway for him to sleep upon. No amount of argument from the servants could dissuade him.

"It pleases me that you are near, My Friend," Kandake said. "I do not trust Tjaty, advisor to the pharaoh."

15

Kandake instructed the servants on the placement of her belongings within her rooms. The women attending her were efficient in their duties, but seemed ill at ease. Kandake put it down to the accusations they had leveled against the Scythian.

"I would like to bathe now," Kandake said. "Is there someone to draw water?"

She was shown to the cleansing chamber. Several tall earthen vessels of water stood about the small space. Upon a shelf hung at shoulder level, set multiple alabaster jars of scented cleansers, oils, and creams. Kandake sampled the contents, rubbing them on the backs of her hands. She made her selection and instructed the women in the removal of her breastplate.

As the breastplate came free sand and bits of debris fell to the floor, but what seemed to astonish the women most was the evidence that Kandake was in fact female. The room was filled with gasps of breath and whispers.

A young girl entered the chamber amidst the clamor. She bent down and began untying and removing Kandake's sandals. Of everyone within the room, the child seemed the most calm.

A woman lifted a water vessel and attempted to pour it over Kandake's form. The stream of water cascaded to the floor with little of it reaching her skin. Kandake turned to discover the reason and saw that the woman was averting her eyes. She stepped into the flow.

The touch of the others meant to assist with her bath was so light that the majority of the sand remained on her flesh. Annoyed at their inept efforts, Kandake completed the ministrations herself— slathering the cleansing creams and oils. During the rinse phases of her bath, she instructed the women to hold the vessels high to pour the water while she stepped beneath the spill.

Kandake squeezed the water from her braids and accepted the hides meant for drying to wipe away the remaining moisture from her skin. As she entered the main chamber of her rooms, the young girl was waiting with her sandals—they had been cleaned, oiled, and wiped dry. She slipped them onto Kandake's feet.

"Thank you, child," Kandake said. "What is your name?"

"I am called Naomi, Princess." Finished tying the sandals, Naomi stood and awaited her next command.

The women collected the clothes Kandake had shed and the skins she had dried with to be cleaned. A woman bent to pick up the breastplate. The manner in which she reached for it displayed a fear of touching the thing.

"That will do," Kandake said. "I will take care of that myself."

"Yes, Princess," she said, relief flooding her face. She left with the other women, all of them scuttling like insects from an overturned stone.

What is wrong with them? She bent to retrieve her breastplate. When she stood, she was somewhat surprised to see Naomi standing there.

"I thought you would have left with the others," Kandake said.

"No, Princess."

Kandake took her breastplate to the cleansing chamber. She swept away the sand that clung to the untanned side of the leather.

"I can do that, Princess," Naomi said. She held out her hands.

Kandake looked down at her sandals. She observed the care and skill the girl used in cleaning her footwear and handed it over. Naomi pulled a small brush from her pocket, sat on the floor, and went to work removing the grains of sand from every portion of the breastplate, including the seams and fastenings. Kandake dragged a bench from the other room. The bottoms of its legs scraped and squeaked as she pulled the seat over the stone floor to sit near the young girl. She patted the bench indicating that Naomi should sit next to her. She clambered up from the floor and took the seat.

"Well, Naomi, it looks like everyone is afraid of me except you."

"I am not afraid." Naomi shook the last of the sand from the breastplate. Rising from her seat, she placed the leather armor in the center of the chamber and poured water over it. After testing the contents of the jars on the shelf, Naomi slathered the leather with her chosen concoction. Following the third rinse she wiped the breastplate as dry as possible.

Fishing around in her pocket the young girl retrieved a bottle of oil, poured a small amount onto the damp skin, and rubbed the entire piece, inside and out. Then she stood it against a wall in the main chamber of Kandake's rooms to dry.

Kandake inspected the armor. She tapped her fingernails on the outside, ran her hand over the inside, and smoothed her fingers over the straps and fastenings. "You have done an excellent job."

"Thank you Princess."

A woman entered the room bearing a tray of food and drink. Her hands shook so badly that the pitchers were in danger of toppling over and spilling their contents.

"I will take that," Naomi said. As the woman handed it to the girl, relief filled the woman's countenance. Naomi set the tray on a low table as the original bearer fled the room.

Kandake inspected the contents of each dish. The pitchers were filled with water, wine, and pomegranate juice, respectively. She selected the juice and poured some into the bronze drinking bowl and drank it down. When she turned, Naomi was staring at her.

"I was quite thirsty," Kandake said. "The desert is very dry."

Naomi nodded and continued to stare.

"Is there a problem?" Kandake asked. *Please do not tell me that you fear those who drink the juices of fruit.* The girl nodded, again. "The juice?" Naomi shook her head in the negative and continued to point.

Kandake observed that the girl was pointing past her and toward the table. She turned her head and caught sight of movement at the edge of her vision. In one steady motion, Kandake took a step forward away from the table and spun around to face it.

A small, brown on brown serpent was making its way across the tray of food. Its underside produced a slight shushing sound as it crossed the stalks of the fresh onion bulbs. Kandake's hand hovered over the snake as it moved. It seemed the creature was more interested in getting away from her than it was in turning to strike.

Her hand matched the serpent's speed in perfect time. She made a quick grab, nabbing it just behind its head. Secure in her grasp, Kandake brought it toward her for close examination. "How did you get here my little friend?" She stroked the back of its head as it coiled about her arm.

"Princess, it did not strike you," Naomi said, wide-eyed.

"Of course he did not strike. This little one strikes nothing larger than himself. I am too large for him to eat."

"Vipers do not eat us, they only care to bring death." Naomi's focus remained fixed upon the serpent.

"He has no venom with which to kill me. This is not a viper, merely a constrictor. He wraps his body around his prey and squeezes until there is no life left within it." Kandake demonstrated by uncoiling its tail and the creature would loop her arm again and again.

"I know it is a viper, one more deadly than the cobra. I heard the sound it made when it was on the table."

Sound? What is she talking about? The animal did not stand or hiss. Understanding came to Kandake. "The sound you heard was the serpent crossing the onion stalks, nothing more. Please, come close and observe."

Kandake uncoiled the snake's body from her arm. She rubbed the scales of its belly against itself several times. "See, no sound. This is not the viper you fear." Naomi came closer, but froze in her track as Kandake extended the creature toward her. "Would you care to hold it?"

"No Princess, please. It will change back if I touch it."

16

Change back? What does she mean, change back? Kandake stared at the young girl. *Change back to what?* She opened her mouth to ask what Naomi meant just as a servant entered the room.

"Princess Kandake," the servant said. "The Pharaoh has granted your request for an audience. He will see you now."

Kandake put on the armband that represented the throne of Nubia, secured the pouch of herbs and medicines about her waist, and left for Egypt's throne room. Outside her door she was met by Shen. It pleased her that he had bathed, changed, and was ready to accompany her.

At the door to the throne room, Kandake and Shen were met by Natasen and Alara. Upon the announcement of their arrival and invitation to enter, Alara walked through the doorway first. He was followed by Kandake with Natasen at her side and Shen followed two strides behind them.

The throne room of Egypt was every bit as spacious as that of her father. The walls were covered in relief carvings of the history of the pharaoh, displaying his lineage to the gods of this kingdom. The walls of Nubia's throne room were covered in the history of its rulers as well. The difference was where Egypt's rulers were connected to their gods, Nubia's rulers were connected to its peoples.

In similar fashion, Pharaoh Nakhtnebef sat his throne with his heir, Prince Khabebesh, accompanying him. In much the same way Kandake did with her father. The difference here was that the prince seemed distracted and inattentive. He presented as one who was bored and desirous of escape, or at the least some type of diversion.

Kandake made one final comparison. That was of Pharaoh Nakhtnebef to her father, King Amani.

Nakhtnebef was every bit as tall as her father, even as broad, but he lacked the presence her father commanded. Something was off. Where was the great pharaoh she had heard so much about, the man that commanded her father's respect that he would lend Nubia's precious resource of warriors to insure Egypt's strength as a kingdom?

Alara began his presentation. "Pharaoh Nakhtnebef, I present to you Princess Kandake, daughter of King Amani ruler of Nubia and future queen of the kingdom of Nubia. King Amani of Nubia extends you the privilege of speaking directly to the throne of Nubia."

At this last, Kandake took two steps forward and sketched a slight nod of her head as the acknowledgement of one ruler to another.

"Princess Kandake," Tjaty Herihor began to speak. Pharaoh Nakhtnebef welcomes you."

"Tjaty!" Pharaoh Nakhtnebef barked. His voice was strong, but strained. "Thank you for your assistance, but I will greet the great throne of Nubia."

Herihor bowed to his ruler and stepped aside. Kandake was certain she glimpsed a look of displeasure on the advisor's face.

Nakhtnebef came to his feet. It was a show of great respect for the throne of Nubia, but Kandake could see the effort and toll it placed upon the man. *There is something wrong here. His countenance and behavior put me in mind of Father when he was ill.*

"Princess Kandake, future ruler of Nubia, thank you for paying this visit. I look forward to the wisdom of Nubia's throne and the strengthening of our alliance." Pharaoh Nakhtnebef fell to his seat more than sat down. The short greeting appeared to claim more energy than the man had to spare.

I am certain that this man is ill. Her hand went to the pouch at her waist. *Healer, please have put in here what is needed.* "Future of Egypt," she turned toward Prince Khabebesh, "the future of Nubia greets you. It is my hope that the alliance between our kingdoms will grow to great strength for our lifetime."

The expression on Khabebesh appeared startled. It was clear that he was not accustomed to being addressed within the throne room, and Kandake was certain that he had not expected her to direct her words

75

toward him. His response was only to appear somewhat less distracted.

Are you truly such a child that you would not attend to the matters concerning a kingdom that you will one day rule? Let us pray that your father's illness does not separate his soul from his body. Egypt has no hope in your rule.

After the end of a very short audience with the pharaoh, two things had become very clear to Kandake. The first was that Prince Khabebesh appeared to lack the wisdom to rule the kingdom of Egypt should his father die. And the second was that it may be best for Nubia to rule this land. She had no desire to see what would become of Egypt and its relations with Nubia should Herihor get to the throne.

Squaring her shoulders and gathering strength from within, Kandake allowed herself the indulgence of one lone sigh before facing the work that lay ahead of her.

_17_

Later that evening the party from Nubia met together to share slices of fruit and a bowl of fresh nuts. The meal with Pharaoh Nakhtnebef, Prince Khabebesh, Tjaty Herihor and other representatives of Egyptian court had been long and difficult. Throughout the banquet Herihor continued to suggest that the pharaoh must conserve his strength, intimating that he should leave him in control of the goings-on, discussion, and whatever decisions would come of it to him.

The area of the courtyard they chose exposed them to the red land of Egypt. Because that part of the desert was barren and hostile, there was no fear of intrusion from this direction requiring no walls or fencing. As there was no structure, plant, or rock to hide behind, it assured the small group there was little chance of unwanted listeners. Even so they spoke in a seldom used dialect of the Nubian tongue. There were times Shen had difficulty keeping up. On those occasions, Alara would substitute a single Scythian word to assist him.

"Things are not well in Egypt," Kandake said. "There is more than the occurrence of illness for this ruler." She took the point of the blade she wore at her side and pierced the skin of the pomegranate. With skill and practice she allowed the escaping juice to spill to the ground, not a wasted drop to stain her clothing. She opened the fruit and poured juice-laden seeds into the palm of her hand and savored the tangy sweetness of each one.

"I agree," Alara said. "He has a blue tinge about his lips. There is no sickness that causes that."

"It is the evidence of poison the healer instructed me to watch for." Kandake forced herself to fill the air around her with light laughter to allay suspicions of what they may be discussing.

"Should the ruler die, will not the son take his place?" Natasen asked.

"You saw him, how he behaved at audience. Would you trust the health, power, and wealth of an entire kingdom to him? He behaves as if he is no more than a child."

"What shall we do?" Natasen asked.

"What Father sent us to do." Kandake cleaned her blade and returned it to its sheath. "You will speak with our warriors and determine the best course of action. Should they remain in Egypt or return to the kingdom."

Natasen bobbed his head in the affirmative. His face took on a determined expression.

She turned to Alara. "You have the most difficult job of all. You must speak with Herihor and learn as much as you can of his plans without him discovering anything of yours. He will be as devious and twisted as an oiled viper and equally as deadly."

"I am young," he said. "I doubt that he will suspect one such as myself to be able to untangle his spider's web of deception."

"Do not be so certain. I doubt that this one waited until he was old to begin his trade as usurper."

At last Kandake turned to Shen who had remained silent throughout much of the discussion. "I need you to find out whatever you can about that Scythian warrior. He may be the only one in Egypt, but I do not believe that to be so. I would know how he fits into this particular puzzle."

Kandake and the others remained in their cluster for a bit longer, continuing their display of enjoying the night air and one another's company. Given an appropriate amount of time, the party disbanded, retiring for the night to their rooms. To continue to avert suspicion, it was decided that whenever they gathered their conversations would be held in the uncommon Nubian dialect.

When Kandake entered her rooms, she found Naomi sitting in the center of the circle of women that had been there to assist with her bath and other needs.

"No! You are wrong!" Naomi was saying. "She is here to help. She would never harm any of us. If we serve her in a worthy fashion, she will bless this kingdom."

The women chattered and clucked their tongues at the young girl. Whatever they were discussing, Kandake could tell that they were in strong disagreement with whatever Naomi was trying to explain. She shifted her weight and the bells at her ankle gave the gentlest of pings.

Alarmed that they had been caught discussing a royal guest, the women returned to their proposed tasks, scattering like so many birds caught pecking at the crumbs of a discarded afternoon meal.

Naomi walked to Kandake. The expression she wore was one of determination mixed with apprehension. "Please Princess Kandake, would you tell them who you really are?"

"Tell them who I am?" Kandake said, somewhat confused by the question. "You know who I am. I am Princess Kandake, daughter of King Amani of Nubia."

"Yes, you are here as the princess, but tell them who you were before you became the princess."

Kandake stared at the child. She felt the eyes of every woman within the room upon her. They were waiting for her to tell them something. She had no idea what that might be, but whatever it was must be very important. *What is this child wanting me to say?* She continued to stare hoping she could in some way decipher what she was being asked.

"I saw you drinking the juice," Naomi declared. "You drank the pomegranate juice."

"Do not others of Egypt drink the juice of that fruit?" *What has that to do with anything?*

"But you drank it when you were angry."

80

Kandake rifled through her memory, trying to search out the meaning of the child's claims. "I do not believe I was truly angry, only a bit disturbed by the behavior of these servants."

"You changed the snake! It would have killed me."

"No, Naomi. That snake was harmless, only a small constrictor."

"No, Princess, I heard its scales rustle. It was a poisonous viper and you changed it. Only the power of a god can do such a thing. You were brought to us from the ground of the people that our god, Ra, loves." She fished in her pocket and pulled out a handful of dirt mixed with sticks and sand. "This fell from your breastplate as you prepared for your bath. We all saw it." Moans escaped the lips of the women around her. "You are Sakhmet, the daughter of Ra!"

Every woman in the room fell to her knees, lowered her covered face to the floor, and trembled in terror. Naomi lowered to her knees, brought her chin to her chest with her arms raised palms up in honor and supplication, but maintained eye contact with Princess Kandake.

18

"Naomi, what are you saying? Please stand, all of you," Kandake said. "I am the daughter of a king, not a god." But they remained where they were.

"We know who you are. Ra sent you to help us. He formed you from the dust of the desert binding you to us. We will serve you. All we ask is that you heal Pharaoh." Naomi's words rushed from her lips.

"Child, I am a warrior that will one day be queen—nothing more." Kandake saw the pleading in the girl's eyes. "But I will do all I can to heal your Pharaoh."

The bowed women sat back on their heels, Naomi lowered her arms. Each gave Kandake their full attention awaiting her command.

Kandake swept her gaze over them. *I thought life would be difficult serving Nubia as their queen. Now I am a goddess?* Kandake took a seat on the nearest bench, exhausted from the long day of travel, but even more from this new development. *This foolishness must end!*

"Shen!" Kandake bellowed.

He bolted into her rooms. The warrior stood at the ready with sword drawn looking about the space for whatever threat he might dispatch. The kneeling women shrieked and trembled at his arrival.

"Spare us, please!" Naomi pleaded, eyes as round as moons. "We will tell no one!"

"There is nothing to tell!" The strength of Kandake's words caused the girl to tremble. She felt a pang of regret for frightening the child. "Shen, I need to speak with my brothers."

"Yes, Princess." He left the room. Every pair of eyes, other than Kandake's, stared after him.

Kandake instructed the servants to leave her alone. "Should anyone ask why you are not with me, tell them I said my guard would attend to anything I need and that you are not to come back until morning."

Natasen was the first to arrive. "What is it? Shen said that I was to hurry."

"You will never imagine what these women believe," Kandake responded in the rare Nubian dialect. "They have decided that I am a goddess, the daughter of Ra!"

"How did they come to that conclusion?" Natasen also reverted to that tongue.

"That is not difficult to understand," Alara said. He entered his sister's rooms with Shen. The four of them sat together on the floor in a tight circle. "The people of Egypt worship Ra. It is said that when he created them, he loved them completely. But the

Egyptians became neglectful in their worship, many turned to other gods."

Alara reached for the pitcher of water and poured a bowl. After taking a sip he passed it around the circle. "Ra was filled with rage. He regretted having ever created them and sent his daughter, Sakhmet, the goddess of war, to slay all of mankind. Sakhmet did just that, but as so much human blood was spilled, Ra's anger was appeased. He asked her to stop, but she was caught in bloodlust and continued to destroy them. Ra mixed a drink from the juice of the blood fruit, the pomegranate, to slake her thirst for blood. The concoction did its work and she allowed the Egyptians to live."

"And they believe that I am this Sakhmet, why, because I am a warrior?" Kandake asked. "Many women of Nubia are warriors."

"That is true, but how many of them wield the power you do?"

Kandake opened her mouth to argue, but Natasen continued.

"Or drink pomegranate juice by the bucket. And there is a story circulating the palace that you caught a deadly viper with your bare hands and changed it to a small constrictor right before your servants' eyes."

"I did no such thing!"

"I do not know, Little Sister," Natasen teased. "You have been known to brandish some great displays of power. I heard that you once conquered a strong Scythian warrior, all on your own. Then there was the time you convinced King Zoskales of Aksum to gift their precious mines to Nubia—and he received nothing in exchange. Everyone knows what great power that would require."

"That is not how it happened!"

Between Alara and Shen, the snickering grew to all out guffaws and Natasen joined them.

"Please! Do not laugh," Kandake said, shaking her brother's shoulder. "These women are expecting that I heal Pharaoh Nakhtnebef."

"Then, Great Sakhmet, you must do just that." The three men were stretched out on their sides in laughter. Alara had tears of mirth streaming from his eyes.

_19_

The next morning a messenger came to Kandake's rooms requesting that she meet with Pharaoh Nakhtnebef. She was led to a small courtyard off the throne room. It was a walled in spacious area, half the size of the expanse that held the kingdoms seat of power. The bricks of the wall were composed of the sand and mud of the desert. The arrangement of the bricks was as much for strength as for beauty. The ground was covered with flagstones made of the same material as the stone of the surrounding walls. Awnings stood in various positions around the enclosure providing shade and protection from the intensity of Egypt's sun.

The pharaoh awaited her arrival upon a couch shaded by one of the large canopies made from fabric of bright colors. Servants came and went through the only other doorway bearing plates of food attempting to coax the pharaoh into eating. He waved them all away as he turned his eyes upon Kandake.

"Princess Kandake," he said. "Thank you for coming. Please come join me."

Kandake settled onto the seat nearest the pharaoh's head. Shen stood post, three strides behind her.

"I trust that the king of Nubia is well," Nakhtnebef said.

"He is well and sends his blessings to the throne of Egypt." Kandake extended a small scroll toward the pharaoh. It bore the seal of the kingdom of Nubia assuring that Kandake had the power to speak for Nubia's throne.

A servant took it from her and handed it to Nakhtnebef. He inspected the seal and scanned what was written upon the rolled sheet. Kandake noted the slight tremor in his hand.

"As you can see," the pharaoh said, "I have not been well. Everything I eat burns as I swallow and brings pain to my stomach. It is as if a great serpent has wrapped itself around my innards."

Kandake held this information in the back of her mind as she extended her regrets for his discomfort. "Have your healers not been of help?"

"No relief they have given lasts more than a day." Just then he appeared to be overtaken by a chill in the air. He shivered as a leaf in a strong wind, but the air was still, hot and dry.

"You sent word to King Amani that you wish for Nubian warriors to remain in Egypt even though the war with Assyria has ended," Kandake said, changing the subject from the condition of his health to the business that brought her to this kingdom.

"The report is that there are problems on the kingdom's south-east border. I am told the unrest is due to Assyrian agitators, men that have failed to return to their homes now that the war is at an end."

The length of the statement appeared to have sapped the strength from Nakhtnebef. He closed his eyes and went still. Kandake waited to see if the ruler would resume his conversation. It put her in mind of the malady endured by her father, but there was something off about it.

Kandake made as if reaching for the scroll of her father that had rolled from the pharaoh's hand and brushed his exposed skin. *The man perspires as if he is burning from within, yet his skin is cool to the touch. Something is very wrong.*

Her touch seemed to have awakened him. Nakhtnebef continued his conversation as if he had never stopped speaking.

"Before King Amani can respond to your request, Pharaoh," Kandake said, "he must be made aware of the warriors' needs and condition."

"I will have a representative brought to you immediately." Pharaoh Nakhtnebef turned to address a servant.

"If it pleases the pharaoh," Kandake interrupted. "Prince Natasen has accompanied me on this journey. He has been instructed by King Amani to inquire of each warrior that he may bring news to their families."

"Yes, of course. Please have him begin at once. I am anxious for King Amani to have his information so that I might have his answer."

"His answer to what, Pharaoh?" Herihor said, coming into the courtyard. He sketched a brief bow to his ruler. "Princess Kandake." He nodded to her as he walked by on his way to Pharaoh Nakhtnebef's side. When his gaze lighted upon Shen, a sneer shaped his lips. The speed with which Herihor erased it, Kandake was almost uncertain she had seen it. "And who is getting this answer?"

"Princess Kandake and I were discussing the retention of Nubia's warriors," Nakhtnebef said.

"Has Egypt's ally consented to aid us?" Herihor fixed Kandake with an assessing glare.

"King Amani has requested that he be informed of his warriors' positions and desires with respect to their extended stay within the kingdom."

"Princess, please inform your king that his warriors are well fed and are willing to perform this service for the throne of Egypt."

"King Amani would hear their words," Kandake said. She looked from the advisor to the pharaoh.

"Of a certainty, Princess," Herihor said. "With your permission, Pharaoh, I will have the captain of your personal guard gather that information at once."

"Tjaty, I have already given permission for a representative of Nubia to do just that." Nakhtnebef appeared to fight off another of his shivers.

"Yes, Pharaoh, but these things must be assessed by one familiar with the needs of a ruler as well as those of a warrior. "This man—" Herihor waved his hand in the general direction of Shen, assuming him to be the representative.

"That is the reason King Amani has designated Prince Natasen to represent him in this matter," Kandake said, interrupting the pharaoh's advisor. "I am certain that you will agree that Prince Natasen has the understanding to interpret the needs of a ruler as well as the knowledge of what a warrior requires.

Herihor's glare shifted from that of annoyance to one of intense hostility. All of which he focused upon Kandake.

<u>20</u>

"Now that the issue of Nubia's warriors is settled, I believe it is best that you rest, Pharaoh," Kandake said. "Would you object to my visiting the marketplace? I have a young cousin I would like to bring an Egyptian treasure."

"I am certain that you will find many things to please a young one," Herihor said through clenched teeth.

Kandake left the courtyard and walked toward her rooms.

"Did you not say that we were going to market?" Shen asked, following one pace behind.

"We are, but first I must tell Natasen about receiving Pharaoh's permission to speak with our warriors." She entered her rooms and found Naomi weeping into a pillow.

"Why do you cry, child?" Kandake asked.

Naomi jumped at the sound of Kandake's voice. She swiped at her face with the tail of her tunic.

"Princess, I was not aware that you were here. Tjaty Herihor said that you were going to market."

"You did not answer my question. What has brought you to tears?"

"It is nothing," Naomi said and busied herself with arranging small figurines across the room.

"Would you mind attending me as I trade? I am hoping to find some small treasure for my cousin. She is about your age and I am certain you would be able to assist me in selecting the proper gift."

"It would be my pleasure, Princess." In her excitement, Naomi turned to face Kandake. A large bruise was purpling on the side of her face.

"What has happened to you?" Kandake asked. "Come to me."

Naomi closed the short distance between them. Kandake took hold of the young girl's chin and tilted her head this way and that, examining the injury.

"Who has struck you?" The edge of anger seeped into her voice.

"No one," Naomi said. She cast her gaze toward the floor. "I slipped in the kitchen and fell down."

"That is interesting," Kandake said, directing her words to Shen. "Did you know that the floors in Egypt have fingers?" She traced the outline of a handprint on Naomi's face with delicate strokes.

The frown of displeasure on Shen's face was evident as was the line of tension that was growing between his brows.

"It is time that we head to market," Kandake said. She removed the armband that represented Nubia's throne, tied her knife to her hip, and left her rooms. Shen and Naomi followed a short distance behind.

Kandake stopped at the entrance to Natasen's room and found Alara with him.

"You have been given permission to speak with our warriors," she said.

"Permission from Pharaoh's advisor?" Natasen asked.

"No, from the pharaoh himself. Herihor would rather have one of his men obtain the information. He was not pleased when Nakhtnebef indicated that you would be the one to speak to them. Be careful, I do not trust that man." Kandake turned to leave his rooms.

"Where are you going?" Alara asked, walking through the doorway.

"I am going to the marketplace. Naomi is going to help me choose a gift for Kheb." She touched her brother's arm. "Now that Natasen has received permission from Nakhtnebef to meet with our warriors, it is best he does it soon."

Alara looked at the young girl and smiled. His gaze halted upon the discoloring bruise on her face. He shifted his gaze to his sister's. When a questioning expression came to his face, Kandake gave him a tight shake of her head.

"She appears to be about Kheb's age," Alara said. "I am certain she will be of great assistance in selecting the proper gift.

"Will you join us?" his sister asked.

"It is tempting. To be in the presence of such a beauty would be an absolute pleasure." Alara gave Naomi a winning smile. She ducked her head in an outbreak of sudden shyness. "But I think it best I accompany our brother. There is much to be heard from our warriors."

Kandake nodded and took her leave for the marketplace.

Outside of the palace, the city of Men-nefer bustled. Everywhere Kandake looked there was new construction taking place.

"It would appear that Nakhtnebef is a productive man." She pointed out several locations of large stone being chiseled, stacked, or moved along the city floor.

"Pharaoh Nakhtnebef is building temples to Ptah, Princess, but do not worry. Many of us remain faithful to your father, Ra," Naomi said. "And there are those that make the pilgrimage to Karnak to your temple, too."

Shen smirked. Kandake would have delivered a sharp elbow to his side had Naomi not be walking between them.

"This way to the marketplace," Naomi directed. "I will take you to the best stalls. But you must be shrewd in your dealing. They will not know who you are and some will try to cheat you."

Kandake allowed Naomi to take the lead. They passed several stands that offered fruits and vegetables. Baskets of fresh and dried spices filled the air with their aromas. Goats bleated in pens and fish were stacked on tables.

"This way," Naomi said. "There is a stall that offers jewels and carvings that I am certain will please you."

Kandake followed. As Shen came around the corner of one of the stalls, his blade caught on the ties of an awning. It came loose causing the fabric to flap in the breeze. Its motion struck the edge of a small earthen vessel and sent it crashing to the ground.

"Hey! You!" the stall owner said, coming from behind his table. "You will pay for that!"

"I have nothing to trade," Shen said.

"What of that?" the owner said, pointing to the copper band.

"Good Sir, this is the ornament of the Sovereign's army. It is not mine to trade."

"You are wearing it. I will have it." Shen made no attempt to remove it from his arm. "You broke my vessel. You must pay. I will take that in trade. Or are you saying that you are a thief."

"A Scythian warrior is no thief," Shen barked. "I serve in the army of the Sovereign of Scythia."

"Then you must pay!" The stall owner reached to take the band from Shen's arm.

Shen pushed the man away from him. He stumbled into his own table and sent the goods on it crashing to the ground.

"Help! Help!' The man yelled until a member of the pharaoh's army came to his aid. "This man has stolen from me and destroyed everything I own!"

21

Kandake attempted to calm the stall owner, but he cried even louder. People in the marketplace began to gather being drawn to the commotion.

"I have not stolen from this man," Shen hissed. "Nor have I destroyed any of his property."

"I must be paid for my goods," the owner complained to the Egyptian warrior who came to quell the disturbance. "Must my family go hungry because this man is a thief?"

"Did you break this man's goods?" the warrior said.

"No, I did not. His awning flapped against one small vessel and it fell to the ground."

"This debris is from more than one vessel." The warrior pushed at the earthen shards with his sandaled foot.

"He knocked the table over." Shen jutted his chin toward the stall owner.

"He did knock over his own table," Kandake said. The crowd around them muttered.

"Princess," Naomi whispered. "This is a dishonest man. He often cries to those who keep order in the market place that he has been cheated when it is not true. He is often the one doing the cheating.

"He pushed me!" the owner shouted.

"Because he tried to remove my armband."

"You must pay the man." The warrior glared at Shen.

"I have nothing to offer him in trade."

"He has the band on his arm. I will take that." The stall owner grabbed at Shen's arm again.

"It is not mine to give." Shen glared at the man until he retreated behind the table of his stall.

"Pay him or you will be bound as his slave until you have paid for all you have broken."

A sly grin slid across the stall owner's face.

"I am no one's slave. I am a Scythian warrior." Shen rooted himself to the ground as the Egyptian warrior attempted to move him into the dishonest man's stall.

"I will pay for the breakage," Kandake said. She reached into her pouch and removed a very small gold ring.

"That will only pay for half," the owner said, eyeing Kandake's pouch.

"That will pay for more than twice the value of all of your goods," Kandake said.

"You cannot tell me what my goods are worth. I set their value!" The stall owner made a grab for Kandake's pouch. "I will have my price!"

"You will have the loss of your hand if you touch me." She laid her hand of the hilt of her knife.

"Who are you to threaten me?" The owner reached for her pouch again.

Kandake took a step backwards and lifted her blade from its sheathing.

"She has threatened me," the man squealed, grasping the warrior's arm.

෴

"That was an experience," Kandake said. The trio walked into the palace courtyard and went straight to Kandake's rooms. Afternoon meal was laid out on a long, low table against the wall and her brothers sat on the floor nearby.

"What experience?" Natasen asked. He popped a brined olive into his mouth and rolled it into his cheek.

Kandake and Shen sat down with them. Once they were settled, servants brought them each a plate piled with the table's offerings.

"A man attempted to make me pay for what he had broken," Shen said. "When I told him I had nothing to trade, he began braying like the nursing colt of a donkey that has been removed from its mother."

"That is not the worst of it," Kandake added. "He called for a peace keeper of the Egyptian army. When Shen said he had nothing for trade he attempted to force Shen into servitude with the stall keeper. I believe that to be his intent all along."

"Why did you not just pay the man?" Alara asked.

Kandake explained the man's greed and his attempt to snatch her pouch. By the time she had finished telling the tale. Both brothers had tears of laughter streaking their cheeks.

"But I was able to find a gift for Kheb." She called for Naomi to bring the bundle of goods from the marketplace.

Kandake pulled two carved alabaster vessels from the sack. The larger urn had streaks of orange brown running through it. The smaller vessel was as white as the clouds of the sky. It was sealed with a well-fitting lid. It took some strength for Kandake to pull it free. The lid came free making a slight popping sound and a tiny cloud of black dust ushered forth and settled upon her hands, lap, and plate.

The men snorted laughter at the surprise and mess. Kandake brushed it off herself and using deliberate motions was careful to spray some of the dust towards each of them. They wiped their hands and continued their meal amongst the merriment.

"No! Princess, you must not eat the food." Naomi batted the food from Kandake's hand and began removing each of their plates. The servants in the room snatched the child away and began swatting and cuffing her for her behavior.

"Stop what you are doing!" Kandake bellowed. The women released the young girl and dropped to their knees, cowering on the floor.

"I am fine," Naomi said. "They did not hurt me."

Kandake called Naomi to her. "Why have you behaved so?"

"Princess, the food is now poisoned. You must not eat it."

"Poisoned? Because of a little kohl dust? The soot of frankincense will not harm us."

"We of Egypt do not use frankincense to make our kohl. We use stib. If you eat it you will die."

22

Kandake picked her plate up from the floor. She sniffed at the dusted food. She pinched a bit of the black powder between her fingers and rubbed them together. "This is truly different than the kohl of Nubia. This does not have the smooth quality nor is it as fine as that of Nubia. It is rough; I can feel the grit of it."

Natasen stared from his sister to Alara and then back to Kandake. "Could—." An abrupt hand signal from Kandake cut his words off.

"I want all of you to leave my rooms, at once," Kandake said, her sharp directive left no room for doubt or dallying. Naomi was the last of the servants to exit. She turned to look at Kandake over her shoulder as she walked. Her expression was one of sadness and confusion.

Once the room was cleared of all but those of Nubia, Kandake took the smallest amount she could of the stib onto the edge of her fingernail. She sniffed at the dust, she could smell nothing. Then she touched it to the tip of her tongue before anyone could stop her and spat it out at once.

Kandake experienced an acute burning sensation on the inside of her lips and the tip of her tongue. She rinsed her mouth with water and spat that back into the drinking bowl. This she poured out the window and smashed the bowl.

"It tastes like the smoke of ironworks," she gasped. She spat again into the bowl shards. "I believe this may be the poison that takes away the pharaoh's strength."

"If you believed it to be poison, why would you put that into your mouth?" Alara growled. "Little Sister there are times when you cause me to wonder at the rightness of your thinking." He stood in front of her forcing her mouth open to examine its insides.

"I did not believe so small an amount to be harmful." She rinsed her mouth again and expelled the contaminated water into her stib-dusted plate. "The inside of my mouth still burns." She rinsed with water once again.

Natasen stood glaring at her. "You have endangered the throne of our kingdom!" He crossed the room and paced back again. "Dangers such as those are for me to take, not my queen!"

"I could not risk you," she said. Natasen opened his mouth to argue, but Kandake spoke first. "You are both correct. What I did was foolish. I should not have risked either of us."

Natasen and Alara continued to stare at her. "You have my word that I will never do such a thing again." Her brothers appeared to be somewhat mollified by her oath.

Kandake rubbed at her middle. Her stomach twisted and constricted in pain. She bolted for the bathing room, fell to her knees, and spewed until her belly was beyond empty.

Shaking and spent Kandake's brothers assisted her to a nearby bench. She yanked free the pouch given to her by Nubia's healer that she kept tied about her waist. Kandake pawed around inside it until she brought out a gray-brown ball about the size of a large nut. "Please, I need a vessel of water and a bowl to grind this in."

Shen brought her both. He set the bowl on the floor and placed the nutlike thing inside. Then with the butt of his knife's hilt he crushed and ground the thing into a coarse powder.

"Pour enough water into the powder until it becomes a thick liquid, like heavy juice," Kandake said. Her voice sounded strained and raspy.

Once Shen did this, she drank the bowl dry. The taste of the mixture was sour and strong, nothing she was eager to endure again. Within moments the knots in her insides untied and released. The swimming of her stomach and head relieved. Even the burning within her mouth ceased.

As she began to feel like herself again she sat straighter and announced, "I know what is causing Pharaoh Nakhtnebef's illness."

23

"I believe someone is putting stib in the pharaoh's food or drink." Kandake stood. She walked to the table where the food was laid out for their meal. She poured herself a bowl of juice and mixed it half with water. After taking a cautious sip she drank most of it.

In the bathing room Kandake rinsed away the bile from the floor. "It is a good thing that my stomach was pretty much empty." She wiped a dampened cloth across her face and neck and forced a smile at her brothers. No one returned it, not even Shen.

"Princess Kandake, this is the first time I have seen you act without wisdom," Shen said. "What if the poison had killed you? How could I return to Nubia and face the king?"

"You and my brothers are correct. I should not have done this. But I needed to know how badly the poison would affect me." She held up her hand to forestall the argument coming from the three. "Our healer in Nubia told me what to look for if I suspected something like this. He also told me what to use to restore the pharaoh's health. Yet, I should not have done that."

"Now that we have this information," Natasen said, seeming somewhat satisfied that she understood his point. "What should we do next?"

"Have you spoken with our warriors?" Kandake asked.

"I have. Many are willing to stay, but there is concern that what their bows will be used for is not in the interest of Nubia."

"They believe Nakhtnebef to be against our kingdom?" Alara asked, his voice colored with astonishment. "We all believed Pharaoh to be Nubia's ally."

"Their belief is that Pharaoh's Tjaty is behind the push for the retention of their services. They also believe that he will use them against Nakhtnebef to usurp his throne."

"What of Khabebesh? Does he not inherit his father's throne?" Shen looked from face to face for his answer.

"He should," Alara said, "If Khabebesh is as immature as he appears, it would take little for Herihor to manipulate or control him; unless Herihor decides to do away with him entirely." Alara poured himself a bowl of water and took a long drink. "I spent considerable time with him while you and Shen went to market. This is a devious man who believes all should fall under his influence. I do not doubt that he would do either of these evil things."

"I agree with Alara. From what our warriors have told me, this is a man whose hunger for power is only matched by his need to cause suffering." Natasen went on to explain what Herihor called discipline for those within his control.

"Has he done these things to our warriors, also?" Kandake asked. An edge came into her voice.

"No he has not. Uncle Dakká took care to place our warriors within their own command as part of the agreement."

"Perhaps it would be best if we gathered our warriors and returned to Nubia," Shen said.

"Then Egypt would be left in the hands of an evil man. Our ally would soon become our enemy." Alara took another drink from his bowl.

"So to protect Nubia," Kandake said, "we must defend Egypt from this viper that has made his nest within this kingdom's throne room." She drank the last of her watered juice. "Before we do anything we must determine if the prince is as foolish as he seems."

Kandake wandered the Egyptian palace with Shen at her heels. Her way was not barred; neither was she questioned about her destination. After straying into several rooms she found Prince Khabebesh within a great space filled with shelves of tablets and scrolls. Stacks of tattered hides and chipped slabs of clay were piled throughout the space, all waiting to tell the story of Egypt's existence.

The prince was seated at a table and appeared to be copying notes from an aged scroll onto fresh sheets of papyrus.

"Good afternoon, Prince," Kandake said, making him aware of her presence.

He turned the sheets upon which he had been writing face down on the table. "Are you lost?" he said. "My father rarely comes into the archives. I believe he is resting in his rooms."

"The truth is that I was looking for you."

"What could you want of me?" The prince leaned back in his seat and put on a face of annoyance. "There is nothing I can offer Nubia. I have no power or position. I am only the pharaoh's son." His expression pulled into a pout.

"And I am the king's daughter. May I sit?" She indicated the chair across from him. Kandake took the seat without waiting for permission. *He is not pleased with his position as Pharaoh's son or is it that he is heir that does not bring him pleasure.*

"What is it you want, Princess?"

"I only wanted to talk. There are few who understand what it means to know that you are the next to rule, few who understand that every choice or decision you make effects so many generations."

"I have no effect upon anyone. I study these scrolls. I learn of this great kingdom and its history, to what end? No one considers my voice."

"But you are Pharaoh's son. I am certain your father wishes to hear what you have to say."

"My father believes that I am a child! He believes whatever Tjaty tells him and he says that I am too young to understand the matters of this kingdom." He rolled and secured the scroll he had been reading and pushed it away from him. "How old are you?"

"I have entered my fourteenth year," Kandake said, not sure why her age should have any importance to the prince.

"Fourteen! And here you are representing the throne of Nubia! I have completed my seventeenth year, and still my father will not discuss important matters with me. But he makes treaties and agreements with a child of only fourteen years!"

The prince's shouting brought guards into the archives prepared to defend and protect him.

"Get out! Get out of here at once!" he screeched at them. "You come to protect me from a girl of only fourteen years! I am no child to be hovered over!" He flung the scroll at their departing backs.

Kandake gave Khabebesh a side-long glare. *You desire to be treated like a man, yet you rage like an undisciplined child.*

"You dare to look at me like that?" he growled at Kandake. "What do you know of a father who behaves as if he will live forever and a Tjaty who plots to take your throne?"

"You are correct, Prince. I know nothing of these things." *So he is not as unaware as he would have the kingdom to believe.* "What I know is that your father will not live forever and Tjaty Herihor can only sit upon your throne if you allow it."

"Allow it?" Khabebesh pushed up from the table "How am I to stop him?"

"Nubia is your ally and would assist you, were you to ask." Kandake leveled her gaze upon the prince's eyes and held them until he resumed his seat.

<u>24</u>

Kandake watched the prince as he appeared to be making a decision. The expressions on his face shifted through multiple changes until it settled into a look of disbelief.

"You are telling me that if I ask for Nubia's aid, you will assist me. If I were to trust you, what could you do for the throne of Egypt? You are a child of only fourteen years. What do you know of ruling kingdoms?"

"I know enough to tell you that what you say of your father's life years is accurate. Unless things change soon, he will not live much longer."

Khabebesh bristled at Kandake's words. His face clouded with anger and pushed to his feet once again.

"I also know that his throne will not pass to you, but to Tjaty Herihor because you have chosen not to become a man, but to remain a child."

The prince slumped back into his seat and placed clenched fists upon the table top.

"I know one more thing, as well," Kandake said. She reached across the table and laid her hand alongside one of his knotted fists. "I am Nubia's future and if I am looking at the future of Egypt the two kingdoms can be allies for a long time to come."

"If it is true that you ruled Nubia during your father's illness," Prince Khabebesh gave Kandake a look of pleading, "is it possible for you to instruct me how to do the same?"

"It can be done, but it requires that many things change and that you be willing to work hard without fear."

"This is something I can do. When shall we begin?" He searched her face as if looking for all of the answers.

"We begin with evening meal. Pharaoh Nakhtnebef has planned a feast for the governors of Egypt's city-states. You must be present and participate in the discussion." She looked about the room. "Do you have much knowledge of your kingdom's history—the works of the pharaohs?"

The prince stared at Kandake in disbelief. "I do nothing but study of Egypt day and night. I abide in the archive, reading and studying the scrolls and tablets looking for a way to strengthen my father's reign." He turned over the sheets of papyrus exposing the copious notes he had taken.

"Good! I will see you at evening meal." Kandake left the archive and returned to her rooms to change for the feast.

She entered her rooms and removed her jewelry in preparation for her bath. Muffled sounds came from the bath chamber. Kandake walked in to discover the source of the sound. She found Naomi curled into a ball on the floor in one of the corners of the room. She went to her.

Kandake lifted her from the corner. "Child, why do you weep? What is—" Her question died in her throat. The sight that met her eyes flashed rage and pity. Naomi's face was swollen and bruised. Someone had beaten the girl and spared no mercy in doing so.

"Who has done this to you?" At her question, Naomi began to wail. Kandake cradled her against her body to soothe the young girl's distress. "Shen!"

The Scythian warrior barreled into the chamber with knife drawn.

"Look at what some animal has done!" She held the girl away from her for the warrior to see the damage done to the child. Kandake rocked and stroked Naomi until her wailing subsided into softened whimpers.

Shen growled words that Kandake did not know, but was sure she understood.

"Please, Naomi," Kandake crooned, "you must tell me who has done this to you?"

As she spoke, the servants attending her came into the room. They saw Kandake holding the young girl and stopped all forward movement.

"Can any of you tell me what has happened to the child?" Kandake looked from face to face, but no one said a word. "I have asked a question. Are the servants in Egypt so devoid of respect that they would refuse a direct order?"

"She was punished for her behavior, Princess," one of the women said.

"Punished? For what crime?' Kandake filled her voice with reproach.

"She was punished because she dared to touch you without permission. She knocked your food to the floor and spoiled your garments." The woman spoke the words with satisfaction as she sneered at Naomi.

"And who administered this punishment?"

"We all did." The face of each woman held a look of pride and justification.

"All of you women beat this one, small child." Rage filled Kandake until she was filled to overflowing. Her breath came to her at a fast pace as if preparing for battle. Her hand moved, of its own accord, to the knife she wore at her side. Her heart said that she must punish these women as they had punished this child. Her mind spoke to her of the discipline of a queen. Everything within her said to ignore the voice, but Kandake knew she must obey it. As her hand gripped the hilt of her blade, Kandake forced herself to return it to its sheath.

Kandake passed the girl to Shen and took enough steps to bring her within striking distance of the women. She spoke in a whisper that assured the hearers of the lethality of her words. "You will leave my sight and never return. For the duration of my visit to Egypt, my eyes must never find any trace of you or you will understand the wrath of a Nubian warrior."

"We must not leave you. Who will tend to your needs?"

"I have my servant." Kandake shifted her gaze to Naomi.

"What shall we say when we are asked why we have left our post?"

"You will say that Princess Kandake, future queen of Nubia, prefers servants that can be trusted, servants that have honor, and servants who will follow my wishes."

The women left Kandake's rooms wailing just the way she had found Naomi.

25

"That should take care of them," Kandake said. "How could women abuse such a valuable resource? A woman, more than anyone, knows the struggle and effort that is required to bring forth and maintain life." She opened her pouch of medicines and knelt down to tend to Naomi's bruises and scrapes. "In Nubia we are aware that children are our greatest resource. Abuse such as this brings swift and terrible punishment."

"It is not their fault, Princess," Naomi said. "They only follow the lead of others."

"What do you mean, the lead of others?" she sat back on her heals.

"It is because of who my parents are. My mother was of Nubia and my father was a Hebrew."

"This was done to you because your mother is of Nubia? Where is she? She left you here in Egypt?"

"It is because my mother is of Nubia that I am able to work in the palace. She was Pharaoh's personal protector. She died during my fifth year of life, but while she lived no one dared to bring me harm, regardless of my father." Pride shown from her eyes.

"Your father?" Finished with the ministrations of the child's wound, she closed and tied the pouch about her waist.

"My father is a Hebrew, that is the reason they mistreat me. He died during my third year." Tears rolled from her eyes. "Egyptians have much to resent about the Hebrews. When they left this kingdom, many Egyptians were pressed into the hard labor they had performed."

"Your father was a laborer?"

"My father was an artisan, he worked gold. He crafted the jeweled collar that Pharaoh wears." She cast her gaze toward the floor. "He made one for me, as well. I wore it every day, but they took it from me the day my mother died." Rivulets of tears cascaded down her cheeks.

"When my mother died, they said that I am no longer of Nubia, that I am Hebrew and everyone knows Hebrews do not own anything in Egypt." Her tears became sobs. "Princess I am of Nubia and I am Hebrew, like my father. That is no reason for them to treat me so."

Kandake swept the young girl into her arms. A mixture of rage and pity coursed through her. *How can a child be treated in this manner. These people may not respect her father, but they must continue to honor her mother. Many things will change in Egypt! I, Princess Kandake, future ruler of Nubia, have pledged it!*

She pushed Naomi away from her in order to grasp her gaze with her own. "Do not concern yourself with what has been done. Today your life has changed. As of this moment you attend me personally. You will assist me in all things. When you are not with me you will be with Shen."

Naomi's face lit like the full moon in a darkened sky. "Thank you, Princess." Her squeals of pleasure and excitement had Shen covering his ears.

"Now that that is settled, it is time to dress for evening meal. Pharaoh has planned a feast in Nubia's honor. Help me dress, please."

As Shen left her rooms, Kandake instructed Naomi in what needed to be laid out in garments and jewels.

☙ ☘

As Kandake left her rooms, she was met by her brothers, Alara and Natasen, both resplendent in formal Nubia attire. The fabric wrapped about Alara's hips was of heavy linen dyed the colors of the Nubian sunset. It was topped by a wide belt of fine-meshed gold woven with threads of copper. Natasen wore a garment of supple, tanned leather about his hips. The hide was nearly the color of his rich dark skin. The pleated center-front of the kilt accentuated his narrow hips and athletic build. Narrow strips of blackened leather woven into a belt circled his waist atop the animal skin.

The upper arms of both Natasen and Alara were encircled by a gold band set with a single stone of lapis, the symbol of Nubia.

Shen wore the dress of an officer of a Scythian warrior—a tunic of black fabric with a mild sheen to its surface. Its length reached to mid-thigh displaying work-hardened muscular legs. The hilt of the blade, worn at his side was made of bronze, but Kandake had no doubt the blade itself was strengthened iron honed to a deadly edge.

Naomi was dressed in a simple tunic of white, but the fabric looked as if it had been dusted with fine gold. Kandake braided her hair as worn by the young girls of Nubia. The ends of the braids of either side of Naomi's face had been coiled with gold wire. At the end of each braid a single bead of lapis had been threaded.

The delicate fabric wrapped about Kandake's hips was of gold spangled midnight and appeared weightless. Instead of a belt, she secured the corners of the fabric in an elaborate knot. At her neck, Kandake draped the Nubian double strand of beads. The wires held alternating globes of lapis and gold. The hue of the fabric and the shade of the beads enriched the luster of her dark rich skin.

Girdling her upper arm was the symbol of the throne of Nubia marking her as its representative, a wide band of engraved gold set with a large stone of lapis etched with the symbol of King Amani.

Kandake surveyed each member of their party. "I believe we are ready," she said. She fell into step behind Natasen and Alara. Shen and Naomi came up behind her, and the five of them walked to the throne room of Egypt.

26

After the announcement of her presence was made, Kandake, and those with her, were led to their seats for the feast. Pharaoh Nakhtnebef sat at the head of the table. Tjaty Herihor sat at his right hand and Prince Khabebesh sat at his left.

Kandake was seated beside Prince Khabebesh, Alara was seated next to her, and Natasen next to him. Across from Kandake sat governors of several of Egypt's city-states. Shen and Naomi stood four paces behind Kandake's chair.

"At last I come face to face with the famous Princess Kandake of Nubia." This came from a governor sitting across from Kandake. "How could one so young and beautiful traipse around pretending to be a warrior?"

"Sir, how is it you know so little of your allies to the south?" Kandake asked. "Nubia utilizes all of its resources, male and female. As for pretending to be a warrior, it is no pretense."

"Then it is true that you will rule Nubia after King Amani," he said. "Does he have no sons?"

"King Amani has two sons," Kandake said. "And they are strong and wise."

The man laughed. "I am sure you are being kind and loyal to your family, but if this were so, would he not have chosen one of them to rule." He nudged the man sitting next to him. The other snickered.

"Fools often laugh when it is clear that they have neither knowledge nor wisdom," Alara said.

"I have heard that said," Khabebesh remarked. He glared at the man who had been speaking to Kandake. "I have also heard that to insult the friend of Pharaoh is unwise as it may lead to unfortunate consequences to one's health and position."

"Prince, I am certain he meant no insult," Herihor said. "I believe he was only remarking at the differences in the cultures of our two kingdoms. Your youth causes you to see slights where none exist."

The prince glared first at Herihor and then at the rude governor. "Is it not the young that bring truth to light and expose the deception of the old?"

"Please, young prince, this is Pharaoh's opportunity to show the nobles that even during his time of illness he has not lost control over this kingdom. How will they believe this if he cannot control his own son?" Herihor hissed to Khabebesh.

The expression on the prince's face was one of frustration and abashment. He made a move as if to leave the table, but Kandake nudged his foot and gave him a tight shake of her head.

"Tjaty Herihor," Kandake said. "Is it not true that as Pharaoh's advisor you are responsible for the prince's training as well?"

"I do the best that I can," Herihor said. He shrugged as if his task was an impossible one.

"You must not be so modest. The conversations I have had with Prince Khabebesh show great understanding for the laws and culture of Egypt." She smiled at his discomfiture. "I can see your tutelage in his grasp of the need for Nubian warriors to return home."

"I do not believe that to be suitable conversation for this time. We would not want to disturb the digestion of these fine men." He made a sweeping gesture that included most of those sitting at the table.

"I would be interested in what the prince has to say," the governor sitting closest to Herihor said.

"As would I," Nakhtnebef said. This was the first time throughout the meal that pharaoh showed any interest or energy.

"Yes, enlighten us, Prince." Herihor gestured for Khabebesh to begin his explanation. He leaned back in his chair. His face pulled into a smug grin.

"Princess Kandake, as our rule of allied kingdoms is likely to run in concurrent periods, I believe it is wise to choose what is best for both." The prince warmed to his subject. "Your warriors have served Egypt well in its time of need. Some have died alongside our warriors which is the ultimate gift to give our Pharaoh. It is a death of honor.

"However, this is a gift that is best offered one's own ruler. In this, King Amani has shown to be a true friend of Egypt. Such friendship must be respected and never abused. Therefore it is my belief that Nubia must have her warriors back."

The nodded heads among the attending governors showed approval for Khabebesh's words.

"Those are lovely sentiments," the advisor said. "But as the young will do, the prince has overlooked a very important fact—the unrest and confusion at our southeast border." Herihor's gaze surveyed the nobles at the table. Their worried expressions were easy for all to read. "With these warriors in place, none would argue the turbulence would soon be put to an end."

Again, the governors' nods assured their support of Herihor's position.

"I fear I must agree with Tjaty," Nakhtnebef said.

"Pharaoh, please indulge me a bit longer." Khabebesh made eye contact with each of the men sitting at the table. He allowed his gaze to linger with Kandake's. She gave him an encouraging smile to continue.

"I believe it would be a mistake to use Nubian warriors for this task for at least two reasons. The first is that using non-Egyptians to regulate or monitor citizens of this kingdom sends a message of weakness of the throne. And second, would that not incite greater disquiet among the people, possibly provoking them to question strength of the kingdom? If Nubia is required to maintain peace and unity within Egypt does that not place the throne of that kingdom above

Pharaoh?" The prince, again, locked his gaze with each governor in turn.

"Please forgive me, Princess Kandake. I do not mean to imply that King Amani has designs upon the throne of Pharaoh." Khabebesh leaned back in his chair as if so much speaking had drawn from the stores of his strength.

"I am not insulted," Kandake said. "Your point is well taken and must be considered. *What you say is the very thing that concerns my father.*

"The boy makes sense," Nakhtnebef said. "Did I not ask you the same thing, Tjaty?"

Herihor shrugged concession to Pharaoh, but the glares he directed toward Kandake and the prince were unmistakable.

Father warned me that you are a dangerous man, Herihor. I will not let that warning go unheeded. Kandake patted the small dagger she wore next to her skin.

_27_

"Princess," Naomi whispered into Kandake's ear while all eyes were on the pharaoh. "Princess, it is important, I must speak to you."

Shen stepped forward and pulled Naomi back to her position behind Kandake's chair. She waited a beat and slipped to Kandake's ear, again.

"Princess it is very important." She stepped back before Shen could remove her.

"I ask your leave, Pharaoh," Kandake said. "It has been a long day."

Pharaoh Nakhtnebef nodded his permission and Kandake rose to leave the table. Natasen and Alara stood to go with her.

At the entrance to her rooms, Kandake invited her brothers in. They seated themselves at the far corner of her sitting room away from the windows and door. Shen sat just outside the circle to better observe for uninvited listeners.

"Now what was so important you had to tell me?" Kandake asked Naomi.

"I know why our pharaoh is ill. If I tell you, you must promise to heal him." Naomi dropped to her knees in front of Kandake. "If you heal him, I promise to make the pilgrimage to your temple and pray. I will even give myself as a priestess."

"Naomi, I am not your goddess."

"I understand I am not supposed to know, but I do. They know too. They clear the way before you." She indicated Alara and Natasen.

"They know no such thing. I am their younger sister, they love and protect me."

"If they are only your brothers, then why do they bow to you?" Naomi folded her arms across her chest and jutted out her chin. A pose that matched the determination she expressed.

"They bow because I am to be their queen. It is an expression of their loyalty to my rule, nothing more."

"Princess I will say what you wish, but I ask that you please heal Pharaoh. He is being poisoned." Tears rolled down her cheeks and made her voice hoarse.

Kandake exchanged glances with her brothers. "What makes you say Nakhtnebef is being poisoned?"

"I saw him do it."

"Who did you see and what did you see him do?" Kandake pulled the girl to her feet so that their gazes met. "It is very important, Naomi, that you tell me exactly what you saw."

"I saw Chatha. That is not his name; it is what Tjaty calls him. Chatha means ends. He is called that because he ends the life of others. I saw him draw on

126

the inside of Pharaoh's drinking vessel. When he pulled his hand away he was holding a rod of stib."

Kandake stared first at Alara and then at Natasen.

"What does this Chatha look like?" Natasen asked. "Can you describe him to me."

The young girl nodded her head. "He looks like him!" she pointed at Shen.

"Shen?" Kandake and Natasen said at the same time.

"You are saying that Shen is Chatha?" Alara asked.

"No, Chatha is not Shen. He looks like Shen. Their eyes and skin are the same.

సా ఎ

Kandake and the others sat talking late into the night. Naomi slept in the area Kandake set up for her within her rooms.

"There is more than one Scythian here," Shen said. "I would have a look at the one they call Chatha." He sat on the floor clenching and unclenching his fists.

"Do you believe you know him?" Alara asked.

"There was one warrior who accompanied the Emissary, he had such talents. He was versed in the art of subtle poisons and assassination. It was the Sovereign's command that he protect the Emissary and the Sovereign's symbol." He made gestures with his hands to refer to the shape of the thing.

"Are you referring to the carved ironstone that I gave to Commander Pho?" Kandake said.

Shen bobbed his head once in affirmation. "The warrior's name was Kuska. One look and I would know him."

Kandake watched as Shen brooded. *Shen is a warrior of great honor. If the man they call Chatha is Kuska, what then?* She let the thought go. "Natasen," she said, gaining her brother's attention. "We have not had an opportunity to discuss your walk among our warriors. What are their thoughts?"

Natasen shifted his focus from Shen. "It appears to be what we believed. Many of them have requested to return to Nubia having fulfilled their pledge. A few would be willing to remain in Egypt, but they have grave concerns."

Kandake and Alara set aside their drinking vessels giving Natasen their full attention. "What concerns them?" Alara asked.

"What many of them have said is that there is little to no unrest within the kingdom. The only Assyrians that have remained within Egypt have severe battle injuries that would not allow them to travel to their home and these men will likely die. There are two that should survive their wounds, but they have lost limbs that will prevent them from returning to any battlefield."

"So what is the unrest that Nakhtnebef requires our warriors for?" Kandake asked.

"There is no unrest," Natasen said. "Herihor tells these things to the pharaoh to cause him fear."

"Does not the pharaoh go into his lands to see for himself?"

"He is too ill to travel very far from the palace." Natasen took a long drink from his bowl. "Many of our warriors believe that Herihor is waiting for the pharaoh to reach a weakened state. At that time he will use the strength and pledge of our warriors to support his attempt to take Egypt's throne."

"And what of the prince?" Alara asked, brooding over his own question, pulling at his lower lip.

"I see it now, Herihor's plan!" he said. "With Nakhtnebef weakened and the prince discredited few of this kingdom would protest the advisor's need to take the throne."

"Whatever the plan is, if Kuska is involved the plan cannot be trusted," Shen said rejoining the conversation. "Evil men are never satisfied with what they have stolen. It would not be long before Kuska or Herihor set their eyes upon Nubia."

"I must agree with Shen," Alara said. "This wickedness must come to an end!"

28

"The only way that will happen is if we put an end to it," Kandake said. She made eye contact with each of the three in turn. Affirming nods came from them all.

"This is a problem we must address from three positions," Alara said, he began to count them off on his fingers. "First, we must address Nakhtnebef's health. Then we must build the people's confidence in Prince Khabebesh. And that brings us to the third and largest problem, exposing Herihor for the usurping jackal that he is, while preventing his use of Nubian warriors to further his plans."

"If this Chatha is Kuska, he must be removed from the situation at once," Shen said. "If he is allowed to move about without restraint, he will continue with his master's plan, only he will become the master."

"But we do not know if Chatha is Kuska." Kandake said.

"That will be my worry," Shen said, fingering the hilt of the long-knife he wore at his side.

"I agree with Alara in that we must see to the pharaoh's health, first." Kandake said. "That task will be for me. If Naomi is correct and stib is being used to ruin his health, our healer has provided me with the necessary means."

"I will work with the prince, but I will need your influence as well, Kandake. It was your words that encouraged him to make his opinions known." Alara gave his sister an approving smile.

"That leaves our warriors for me to deal with," Natasen said. "I am certain they will follow me in this situation as they would Uncle Dakká. They will also assist me with the containment of Tjaty Herihor."

They discussed their strategies further, offering and receiving suggestions about details of the execution of their plans. This continued until just before daylight at which time they adjourned to their own rooms. Kandake slipped into her bed to sleep for a few hours before starting her day.

๑๑ ๙

"Princess, Princess," Naomi called from the foot of Kandake's bed. "Pharaoh has asked for you to attend him."

Kandake stretched and executed a wide-mouthed yawn. She turned to look out of her window to check the position of the sun. It was climbing toward the seventh hour of the day.

"Oh, I did not intend to sleep this long." She climbed from her bed and walked to the room for her bath. When she entered the booth, tall vessels stood around the walls filled with clean cool water.

Naomi clambered onto a short chest. She struggled to lift one of the tall jars to pour the water over Kandake.

"Let me help you with that," Kandake said.

"But Princess, it is my job. I can do it."

"It is your job, but no one truly works alone. A ruler requires the assistance of an advisor and his citizens to create a strong kingdom. No warrior conquers an army by himself. And today you and I will lift the jars, together, for my bath.

Once the bath was complete, Kandake squeezed the excess water from her braids and gathered several of them back from her face. She tied them with the gift she received from Amhara that was both a decorative piece and a weapon. Then she slathered creams and oils over her skin.

Naomi assisted draping and tying a length of colorful fabric about her hips. As the young girl fastened a string of carnelian beads at the back of Kandake's neck, Kandake slipped the small blade she wore next to her skin within the folds of the skirting fabric. With the last twitch to the fall of her skirts, she left her rooms to begin her day.

She entered the palace courtyard hoping to find Nakhtnebef. She spied a large canopy and walked toward it thinking she would find him there. Much to her displeasure, Kandake found herself in the company of Herihor, advisor to the pharaoh.

"How is Pharaoh Nakhtnebef fairing today?" Kandake asked, attempting to cover her irritation.

"Pharaoh is having a better day," Herihor said. "He is in the temple delivering an offering to Ptah."

"Thank you," Kandake said and turned to leave.

"Might I inquire where you are going?" he asked.

"I am going to the marketplace." She gave him a look she hoped would discourage him from asking further questions.

"Please forgive my intrusion, Princess, but I understand there was some difficulty on your last visit there. Allow me to have a servant to acquire whatever it is you need."

"Thank you, but I am not certain what it is that I wish to procure, you see. It is a gift for my father. My protector is accompanying me, so all will be well."

"I believe your protector was the source of the difficulty. I will send one of Pharaoh's personal guards to be certain there is no further incident."

"That will not be necessary." Kandake walked toward the doorway through which she had come to conclude the discussion.

"I insist, Princess."

Kandake stopped walking, but did not face him.

"I could not allow anything untoward to happen to the daughter of such a valued ally. Chatha will meet you at the palace gates with one of Pharaoh's chariots."

You are up to something. What is it? What do you not wish me to discuss with Nakhtnebef?

133

29

"Princess Kandake," Shen said. "I do not trust this man. He is sending an assassin with you to the marketplace."

"I do not trust him, either," she said.

"Then perhaps we should not go. Or at least wait until Natasen is free to go with you."

"I must speak with Nakhtnebef and this opportunity to do so away from the palace could not be better. Natasen must spend as much time as is needed with every one of our warriors. It is vital that he ensure their allegiance to the throne of Nubia, alone." She placed her hand upon Shen's shoulder. "You will be with me. Whoever this Chatha may be, he will not overcome the skill of the warrior of Scythia's Sovereign. And do not forget, the skill of a Nubian warrior will be added to yours."

Kandake exited the palace entrance. Before her stood a long chariot decorated with gold and precious jewels. On its sides were the emblems of Pharaoh Nakhtnebef. The driver of the rig wore a kilt of fine linen and a beaded collar marking him as a servant who worked within the palace. Next to him stood a man that possessed the same features as Shen—straight dark hair, skin of honey brown, and eyes that appeared as if they had been pulled from the sides. This was Chatha, the man Herihor insisted accompany her and this man was of Scythia.

Kandake looked to Shen. The tight nod of his head and the grim set of his jaw assured her that this was the dreaded assassin of his sovereign, Kuska.

Chatha stepped from the deck of the chariot to assist Kandake's entrance. When Shen made to climb in behind them, Chatha blocked his way.

"This coach is only for the princess," Chatha said. "You and the child may run along behind."

"Shen, and the child, ride with me," Kandake said.

"Princess, my orders are for you to be carried alone." He glared at Shen.

"Shen is my personal protector and she is my personal attendant. They are with me always."

"I am here for your protection. If you want him near, he may run alongside." Chatha and Shen locked gazes with matching sneers.

"My protector rides with me or I do not ride," Kandake said, and moved to leave the chariot. Shen extended a hand to assist her descent.

"Princess, if you will tell me what it is you wish from the market, I will obtain it for you?"

"You misunderstand," Kandake said. "My plans have not changed. I am going to market. It was never my desire to be carried there." She stepped around the horses and proceeded toward the marketplace at a brisk pace. Shen did a poor job of disguising the grin the crept across his face.

"Kuska is not accustomed to having his wishes denied," Shen said. "He will not be happy."

Kandake turned to see the man barking orders to the driver and scurrying to catch up to them.

"Princess, no one ever denies Chatha," Naomi said, looking behind them. The lines of worry inscribed themselves upon her features. "When Chatha comes, will your father protect you?"

"My father is far from here," Kandake said. "The king must remain in Nubia. Shen and I will manage one man."

"I mean your real father, the great god, Ra." She looked at Kandake with eyes filled with expectation. "If Chatha attacks you, will Ra come?"

"I am the daughter of King Amani of Nubia." She lowered herself to be on eye-level with the young girl. "I have no other father. But, if it is Chatha's desire to measure himself against a Nubian warrior, I will teach him what I can."

Naomi's face was filled with confusion and worry.

"Please do not worry yourself, young one," Shen said, taking Naomi's chin in his hand. "If Kuska means the princess harm, I will see to it that it does not happen."

She turned sorrowful eyes upon him. "Please protect the princess, Ra has sent her to heal my Pharaoh, without her he dies."

30

Kandake rose from the ground just as Chatha joined them. She brushed the dust from her skirts and resumed her direction toward the market. Shen and Naomi took their places on either side of her forcing Chatha to walk behind. Again, Shen appeared hard-pressed to keep mirth from his expression.

Kandake wandered from stall to stall examining first one item and then another. The party had traversed nearly the entire expanse and had not yet made a purchase.

"Princess, if you will tell me what you are seeking perhaps I may direct you," Chatha said.

"There is nothing for me to tell you. I will know it when I see it." Kandake continued to the next stall.

The far side of the marketplace was bounded by the temple of Ptah. Kandake had a merchant to unfurl a carpet just as she spotted Nakhtnebef exiting the temple. "This will do," she said to the owner of the stall. She passed her pouch to Shen for him to pay the man as she aimed herself toward the pharaoh. As she came nearer to him, Chatha blocked her path.

"Princess, Tjaty has asked that I limit you to the market, an area in which I can keep you safe."

"Please do not worry, I will be fine." She stepped around him.

"I have my orders," he said and placed himself in her path, again.

"Yes you may, but they are not mine." Kandake walked around him, again. By now Shen had finished his exchange and brought the rug to Kandake. The pharaoh's chariot was passing within an easy distance to be hailed. Kandake raised her hand to gain his attention.

"Princess, Pharaoh Nakhtnebef is not to be disturbed," the Scythian assassin said, reaching for her hand and pulling it down.

"Your hands must never be placed upon me." She shook him off of her, affronted by such audacity. She raised her hand again, but this time she called to Nakhtnebef as she did so.

"Princess, I will not tell you again." He reached for her. Before he could make contact, Shen had grabbed hold of his arm.

Chatha turned and plowed his fist into Shen's face. Shen matched his blow and Chatha's nose split open and ran with blood. Kandake heard a decided crunch and watched as Chatha went at Shen with fury. He rammed his forearm into the side of Shen's neck. Shen staggered sideways and stumbled, threatening to lose his feet. He took hold of the opening of Chatha's shirt and brought him down with him.

Should Kandake assist her friend and insure the assassin's defeat or should she gain the pharaoh's attention and accomplish her task of creating obstruction to Herihor's designs on an ally's throne. Nakhtnebef's chariot slowed as it came upon the disturbance in the marketplace.

The Scythians rolled in the dust trading blow upon blow. Chatha appeared to be gaining the upper hand of the conflict. He sat upon Shen's middle and pulled a short blade from within his kilt. He angled the knife's edge to slice across the throat of his adversary. Shen grabbed hold of Chatha's sinewy arm halting its progress.

Kandake tore her eyes away to track the chariot's direction. It was coming right at her. Her gaze swung back to the struggle and riveted upon the blade. It moved toward its target once more. Shen strained to stop it again, but it kept going. His arms trembled from the exertion. Kandake was hard-pressed to maintain her distance. Her heart wanted, no, needed to aid her friend. She gripped the hilt of the knife worn at her side. Everything within her screamed for her to yank it from its hiding place. It would take little effort for her to gain control of the assassin while Shen had him engaged. As the knife's edge created a bright red line across Shen's neck, the temptation to interfere was almost overwhelming. *No!* she chided, *Shen is a capable warrior. You will not bring shame to him or the throne of Nubia by such an act.*

Just as she could bear to watch no more, Shen arched his back to an acute angle. Chatha's arms lowered as if he would succeed in cutting the warrior's throat, but Shen's knee came up with a force that propelled the assassin's body over his head and onto the ground behind him. Shen scrambled to get on top of Chatha and pounded the assassin until he lost consciousness. He rose, stepping away from the still form and mopped at his cuts and scrapes.

The pharaoh's chariot halted before the commotion caused by the brawl. "What is going on here?" the pharaoh asked. He looked to Kandake for an explanation.

"Pharaoh Nakhtnebef, if I may have a word," Kandake said, "it would be my pleasure to explain." Nakhtnebef nodded and beckoned for Kandake to join him in his chariot.

"This man endeavored to prevent my communicating with you. So intent was he that he attempted to grasp hold of my person." Kandake pulled herself up to her most regal posture. "My protector intervened and the altercation ensued. The results are as you see."

Appalled at the man's behavior, Nakhtnebef commanded his guards take the unconscious Chatha into custody. "Why would he not wish you to speak to me?"

He studied Kandake for a long time. She bore his scrutiny well having had long practice of such inspection by Uncle Dakká as Prime Warrior and she as his apprentice. "You have the look of truth about you," the pharaoh said. "Share evening meal with me. I would hear more of this encounter."

"It would be my pleasure to do so," Kandake said. "But I must insist that my personal attendant prepare and serve our meal."

Nakhtnebef directed his gaze toward Shen.

"Shen is solely my protector." Kandake focused her attention upon Naomi. The young girl stood tall, squaring her shoulders.

"This child is your attendant?" he asked.

"Naomi has served me well since my arrival in Egypt. I would have no other." Kandake watched the smile spread across Naomi's face and the light of pride come into her eyes.

Nakhtnebef stared at the young girl. "She puts me in mind of my own protector of some years ago. She died and I have found no one to take her place."

"That protector was my mother," Naomi said.

_31_

Kandake entered her rooms upon return from their venture to the marketplace. She refreshed herself with watered juice and honeyed figs served by Naomi. At Kandake's request, Natasen and Alara joined them.

"Chatha is the assassin Kuska?" Alara asked, looking from Kandake to Shen.

"He is," Shen said. "And I will return him to Scythia to face the Sovereign."

"How will you manage that?" Natasen asked. "He is being held by Nakhtnebef."

"It is my duty. I will take him before the Sovereign." The expression on Shen's face shifted to one of stone. He folded his arms across his chest and gave a solitary nod of his head—a sure sign that there would be no convincing him to do otherwise.

"How was your time spent with Khabebesh," Kandake asked Alara, changing the subject.

"It was exhausting, to say the least. We discussed everything from Egyptian history that I was familiar with and much that I was not. It appears you have roused a nest of hornets, My Queen." Alara accepted a vessel of watered juice from Naomi. "Khabebesh has a love for this kingdom and desires to implement plans of his own to build her strength."

"Has he presented any of these to his father?" Kandake asked.

"He has attempted to do so, but at every turn Herihor has explained to pharaoh why they would not be in the best interest for the kingdom."

"What do you think of his plans?" She passed the bowl of brined olives to Alara. He declined and went on to answer her question.

"Many of them are sound and a few of them would also be in the interest of Nubia, were they carried out." He selected a honeyed fig, popped it into his mouth, and continued speaking after he chewed and swallowed the sticky fruit.

"It is certain that he is not the idle child that he has been portrayed to be. Nakhtnebef would do well to hear him." Alara wiped away the honey from his fingers.

"That is my experience of him as well. The night of our arrival and first audience with Pharaoh Nakhtnebef, the prince presented as someone without wisdom or interest in this kingdom. Yet, when I spoke with him privately, his passion for Egypt was very clear." Kandake plucked another olive from the dish. "It did not take much encouragement to get him to speak up at the feast."

"That was your doing?" Natasen asked. He peeled a pomegranate and chewed its seeds. "Our warriors have reported the prince spending time in their camps. He has asked several to assist him with the accuracy of his bow."

"What is the perception of our warriors with respect to Nakhtnebef's request?" Kandake asked.

"Many of them do not believe their services are needed here."

"What of the reports of unrest and the Assyrian agitators?" Alara asked

"There is the usual confusion and fear that follow after a battle, but nothing beyond that. The Assyrian presence is what I told you before, the severely injured with no means of returning to their home. These are not stirring up trouble. They are hoping to remain in Egypt without prejudice."

Kandake sat pondering the facts she and her brothers had gathered. She had the information her father had sent her to obtain, but she could not return to Nubia with things the way they stood.

Egypt is not in danger from its citizens. I see no threat of civil war. The only danger here is that which comes from Herihor. But how deeply does his threat run?

This situation is like watching the waters of the Nile. Its surface may appear calm and peaceful, but there is death lurking beneath. Herihor is a crocodile waiting to devour the throne of Egypt. I do not believe his feeding upon one throne will satisfy him. To that vile creature, Nubia must look like a tasty morsel.

32

Kandake looked at her brothers, and gathering strength from their presence she came to a decision. "We have the information father sent us to gather. However, I do not believe we can leave, yet—at least not with things the way they stand in Egypt. As long as Herihor has Egypt's throne within his reach, Nubia is not safe."

"I am in agreement," Alara said. "But I do not see how we can make any changes without threatening the peace between the two kingdoms."

"Princess," Shen said. "My arm and my weapon will stand with you always, but I have the same opinion as Prince Alara. If we attack Herihor, or any of Egypt, it will be seen as an act of war."

"That is why none of us will attack him, or anyone. Instead, we will strengthen Nakhtnebef and the prince." She warmed to her subject. "I have promised Father and Naomi that I would do all that I am able to restore the pharaoh's health and I believe I have the means to do so. Once his health has returned, I doubt he will be so easily swayed by his advisor."

She turned to Alara. "If the prince responded to a small amount of encouragement…."

"What would he do if someone were to encourage him further?" Alara said. His eyes lit with the excitement that rode within his sister's voice. "I am certain the prince would speak up more often and if the pharaoh's strength is returned, he would have to listen to the words of his son."

"I can make certain that our warriors only follow the commands of the Nubian throne. If I am among them, they will follow my orders and none that come from Egypt, regardless of who speaks them. For my words to contain their greatest strength, I must move into the camps."

"I will see what I can find out about the Scythian warriors that are in Egypt," Shen said. "Those who fear the work of Kuska would follow him rather than die the horrible death he could deliver. His imprisonment may allay some of that fear. If they feel outside of his reach they may turn their hearts toward the Sovereign."

While they spoke among themselves, Naomi busied herself with tidying Kandake's rooms and filling the pitchers with cool water. Kandake called the young girl to her.

"Please ask Pharaoh Nakhtnebef if I may take evening meal in the courtyard."

"Yes, Princess." Naomi scurried off to deliver her message.

When her brothers looked at her with questions written over their faces, Kandake said, "We know Nakhtnebef is being poisoned with stib. We also know who has been doing it and Naomi has told us how." She bounced the pouch of medicines on her hand. "Now we begin restoring health to the kingdom of Egypt. Let us begin with the throne."

"Pharaoh Nakhtnebef, thank you for allowing me to share this meal with you in this beautiful space." Kandake sat in the chair provided. "Please, may I ask you indulge me one more thing?"

"What might that indulgence be, Princess Kandake?" Nakhtnebef asked.

"That you permit my attendant to serve the meal following a particular ritual in which I have instructed her." Kandake beckoned Naomi to come stand before the pharaoh. "Her mother once served you. Naomi is eager to demonstrate her value to you as a servant of your palace."

"How could I deny such a request?" Pharaoh said. "One so young and yet eager to prove her value. Naomi, you are very much like your mother, indeed. Our meal is in your hands."

The young girl bowed her respect and appreciation for the pharaoh's complement and set about fulfilling her task. She placed a large bowl in the center of the floor and filled it with clear, clean water. Naomi gathered the dishes upon which the meal was to be served and removed them from the table. These she placed with in the bowl of water and scrubbed them clean. Once clean she laid them out before Nakhtnebef and Kandake.

She emptied the bowl and refilled it with more water. Now she rinsed every piece of fruit and served these on the clean dishes set for the meal.

"Why does she do this?" Nakhtnebef asked. "Does she believe my kitchens are not clean, that my servants would serve me unclean fruit?"

Naomi froze in her tracks, looking to Kandake on how to proceed.

"Please do not be offended, Pharaoh. Allow Naomi to care for you." Kandake motioned for the girl to continue.

She poured water into their drinking vessels and waited for them to begin their meal.

"This young one has gone to a lot of trouble to prepare a meal that, much to my regret, I will not enjoy." Pharaoh sipped his water with caution. He stared at the vessel, then sipped again. He set the water aside and stared at it with wide eyes.

"Is there something troubling you, Pharaoh?" Kandake asked.

"Not at all!" he said. "This is the first sip that I have had that has not caused pain or burning." He raised the vessel again and drank deeply. He laughed out loud and slapped the container to the tabletop. "You," he pointed to Naomi, "refill my vessel!" He gulped it down and laughed again.

"I am told the dates of Egypt outshine those grown anywhere," Kandake said and popped one into her mouth. "They have spoken the truth!" she said and reached for another.

Nakhtnebef nibbled the end of the dark, sweet fruit. A look of extreme pleasure crossed his face. He pushed the rest of the fruit into his mouth and chewed in contented gratification. He ate a few more dates then gripped his belly in a display of discomfort and spewed what he had eaten.

_33_

"Pharaoh Nakhtnebef!" Kandake reached for the ruler to support him as he slumped in his seat. "What is it?"

"It is my inward parts. I had thought the trouble to be at an end when I could eat without the pain or burning. But I was incorrect." His breath came in short pants as obvious signs of pain passed over his face.

"Shall I call a healer?" she asked.

"My healers have done what they can. The trouble returns with the next meal." Beads of sweat formed on his forehead and upper lip.

"Then might I offer a Nubian remedy?" At his nod Kandake removed the pouch of medicines she wore at her waist. "Naomi, bring me a grinding stone."

When the girl returned with it, Kandake directed her to cleanse it like she did their dishes. Then Kandake removed a nut-gall from the pouch and

151

ground it into a fine powder. She poured the dust into pharaoh's vessel, added water, and mixed the potion.

"Pharaoh Nakhtnebef, you must drink all of it." She handed the drink to him as the pain appeared to subside.

"Ugh, what is that?" he said, pushing the drink away after his first sip. "This is most foul-tasting."

"The taste is not to please you, but to heal you." Kandake held the vessel to his lips and tilted it for him to drink, as he sipped and spluttered through every drop.

"Why must healers concoct the most unpleasant devices," Pharaoh said as he swallowed the last drop. After a time he released his grasp of his middle and straightened in his seat.

"Naomi, Pharaoh Nakhtnebef requires another drink of water."

She took his vessel from the table, cleansed it and refilled it with cool water. He took the water from her and drank with greed.

"My stomach calms," Nakhtnebef said. "How is it that I can now drink water without ill effect, but simple foods, like dates, vex me?'

"I believe the dates will no longer trouble you," Kandake said. She offered him the fruit.

Nakhtnebef took one and nibbled with caution. He looked to Kandake and she encouraged him to continue. He chewed, swallowed, and sat as if waiting for the pain to return. When the pain did not return, he ate another—again no pain.

"How I long for a slice of meat," Nakhtnebef said. His servants bustled to prepare a plate stacked with slices of meat and cheeses.

"Please allow Naomi to continue her service to you." Kandake instructed Naomi to prepare the meal as before—cleansing the dish first then adding the food. She placed it before her pharaoh.

Nakhtnebef tore a small morsel from the corner of a slice of the meat. He chewed it with care, savoring the moment. He appeared to be waiting for the pain to return. After a time, he shoved an entire slice into his mouth. He chewed with relish. The meat's juices dribbled from the corners and down his chin.

Uproarious laughter burst from him. He laughed so hard he began to choke on the huge mouthful. Kandake held a bit of linen before him like a mother to a child bidding him to give up what he chewed. He shook his head in the negative refusing to relinquish the food and kept chewing. His behavior required Kandake to administer a sound pounding on his back to relieve his coughing fit.

Half of the mouthful flew from his lips. He swallowed the rest in a huge gulp.

"That was worth every blow," Nakhtnebef told her, laughing and gasping for breath until tears formed in the corners of his eyes.

After the evening meal, Kandake returned to her rooms within the Egyptian palace to consider how she should tell Pharaoh Nakhtnebef about the poisoning. Alara joined her.

"Have you told the pharaoh of your suspicions?" Alara asked. He took a seat within her sitting room. Naomi brought him something cool to drink.

"Not at this time. I did administer the antidote of nut-galls. According to what our healer told me, I will need to make certain he receives no more stib and administer the remedy several more times to complete his healing." She leaned back in her seat, tired from the long day. "Have you spoken with Prince Khabebesh?"

"We shared evening meal." He took a sip of his beverage. "He has studied much of Egypt's history and spent much time observing the manner in which his father rules the kingdom. He says the Tjaty discourages any discussions with his father on matters pertaining to the kingdom."

"Is that so?" Kandake sat forward in her seat. "It appears to me that Herihor is positioning himself to rule should anything happen to the pharaoh." A long yawn escaped her lips. "In the morning, I will request Nakhtnebef take me on tour of the kingdom. That will keep him away from the palace for at least two meals. I can also give him another remedy before I must tell him of the stib."

"I will do the same with the prince, but for very different reasons." He rose from his seat. "Sleep well, My Queen. Tomorrow promises to be a very long day."

Naomi laid out the clothes Kandake would sleep in. She helped remove the jewelry and placed it upon the dressing table.

"Princess, may I ask you a question?" Naomi asked as she turned back the coverings on Kandake's bed. Given permission, she asked, "Will you be able to save my Pharaoh?"

34

One of the guards assisted Kandake into Pharaoh Nakhtnebef's chariot. She stood beside Egypt's ruler. Another of his guards acted as driver and urged the horses forward. Naomi rode in the short wagon following them. It carried the meals they would eat while touring the land. The day was hot and the air quite dry. Before traveling very far a canopy was erected over the pharaoh's chariot shielding him from the punishing rays.

"Take us outside Waset," the pharaoh said, directing his driver. He turned toward Kandake. "While there are the beautiful temples and the marketplace within the city, the beauty of Egypt is in its people."

The chariot moved along the outskirts of Waset. Kandake saw potters working a large pit of clay. Women washing clothing as groups of children played nearby.

As they traveled, the chariot passed a young boy driving a small flock of geese. Their black tail feathers twitched back and forth as they walked. A large gander, toward the rear of the bunch, took an interest in something in the dust. He stopped to peck it from the ground. Another male took the same interest and went after the same item. A squabble of hissing, honking, and wing flapping ensued. A flurry of pink bills delivered nasty pecks and pinches. Before the boy could separate them, a cloud of red-brown feathers filled the air around them.

"They are a noble bird and much loved of the gods, but their temperament is most quarrelsome and fickle," Nakhtnebef said. "I wonder if that is due to the close association with our deities?"

Kandake could suppress her giggle but not the smirk that pulled at her face.

"Driver, stop up here." Nakhtnebef stood once the chariot came to a halt. He eased himself down and walked toward the center of a grouping of small homes. "This is the settlement I wanted you to see," he said. "The citizens that live here are planting flax. Though the crop belongs to the throne, these families get a share of the linen that is produced."

The people living in the small area gathered as near to the pharaoh as they dared, watching and listening to what was said.

Kandake walked to the far edge of the modest village. "I can see the boundary of the flood waters of the Nile. This will be good ground for your crop."

"Princess Kandake," Naomi called as Kandake and the pharaoh walked back toward the chariot. "May I set up for your meal? It is long past midday."

Kandake looked toward Nakhtnebef, at his nod she directed the young girl to prepare their food. "I believe it would be good to include the people of the village. It would give them something to celebrate."

"It would also give their Pharaoh an opportunity to know them better." Pharaoh Nakhtnebef stared at Kandake for a long moment. "I am beginning to understand why you were chosen to follow your father's rule."

Naomi, Shen, and one of the pharaoh's guards began setting up tables for the meal. Residents of the settlement brought food to be shared. After all was collected and laid out, Naomi gathered the plates and drinking bowls to be washed as Kandake had instructed.

A crash of dropped dishes followed by a yelp of pain could be heard coming from the wagon. One of the pharaoh's guards came striding toward Kandake and Nakhtnebef all but dragging Naomi in his wake.

He tossed the young girl at the feet of his pharaoh. "This Hebrew's spawn was found touching the dishes Pharaoh is to eat from."

"What is the harm?" Nakhtnebef said. "She is preparing our meal"

"Tjaty said no one is to handle these other than to place your meal upon them." He turned to kick at the girl. "Not only did she dare to touch them, I found her piling them in a vessel and pouring water over them as if Pharaoh's bowls needed to be cleansed."

Kandake left her seat to stand between Naomi and the guard. "She attends me and only does what I instruct her to do. Do not touch her again." Kandake glared at the man.

"She is but a Hebrew orphan. She has no worth." The guard spat on the ground.

"She is a child, therein is her value! Without children the kingdom dies. If her father is Hebrew, then she comes from a great people with an even greater god. Her mother is of Nubia and I am told she was a great warrior. That makes this child the product of two great peoples. Her mother is not here to speak for her, but I am. If you harm her, all who know you will mourn their loss."

"Pharaoh," he pled. "I was instructed to protect these items. Tjaty fears that someone may try to poison your meals."

"You believe this child is trying to poison Pharaoh Nakhtnebef," Kandake said.

"Maybe not the child," he said.

"Then is it the people of this village that are trying to poison their pharaoh?" She swept her hand toward those gathered around them. Several that heard her words gasped. The others muttered.

He shook his head in the negative and glanced around him.

"That only leaves the throne of Nubia to be under the suspicion of the pharaoh's advisor." Kandake locked her gaze onto that of the guard. He seemed unable to look away, but his shoulders fell as if he had betrayed a confidence that he had not intended.

"This has gone far enough," Nakhtnebef bellowed. "Nubia has come to Egypt by my request. The throne of that kingdom has been ally to the throne of Egypt for many generations. There is trust between the two kingdoms. There is no poison directed toward the throne of Egypt."

"But I am afraid there is," Kandake said.

35

"There is poison directed towards the throne of Egypt," Kandake said. "But it does not come from the throne of Nubia."

"Princess Kandake, what are you saying?" Pharaoh Nakhtnebef was on his feet. His gaze riveted from Kandake to the guard, then back to Kandake, again.

"I have much to say about this, but it is not for the ears of your people." Kandake looked out over the planting field toward the Nile. "Shall we walk?"

Kandake and Nakhtnebef strode out over the field with Shen and the pharaoh's guard accompanying them. They stepped a short distance from them so their conversation would not be overheard

"I believe there is someone within Egypt that means you harm," she said, once they had reached the center of the field. "I am not certain that one means to kill you, only weaken you."

"What are you saying?" the pharaoh asked. "Do you know who this person is?"

"Naomi observed the one called Chatha draw on the inside of your drinking vessel with stib. To draw a few lines is not enough to kill you, but it is sufficient to cause you the illness you have suffered."

"I will have him executed!" Nakhtnebef shouted. "He will die this day!"

"That will not put an end to the threat," Kandake said. "Chatha is only a tool. He follows the orders of another. You have Chatha imprisoned, but for the threat to be at an end, you must cut off the hand that wields the tool."

"Tell me the name of this jackal!" the pharaoh demanded.

"I am not truly certain," Kandake said. "I suspect, but before I say a name there must be no doubt. You requested the assistance of the throne of Nubia and King Amani has sent us to aid you."

"You speak with wisdom." Nakhtnebef paced back and forth within the field. "To end treachery such as this, one must remove the serpent's head."

"My brothers and I will continue to watch. In the meantime, you must clean your dishes before eating anything." She passed him several of the nutgalls from her pouch. "Should you feel your illness return, grind up one of these, add the powder to water, and drink the mixture. It will render the stib ineffective."

"Thank you for your assistance," he said and tucked the nutgalls into the folds of his belt. "It is best we discuss this with no one until the jackal has been caged. Nubia is Egypt's ally."

ço eð

Kandake returned to her rooms within the palace
following her outing with Nakhtnebef. She sat with
Naomi telling her about the warriors of Nubia and the
training they must undergo.

"Do you believe my mother did this, too," the girl
asked.

"If your mother was a Nubian warrior, I am
certain of it." Kandake brushed her braids over her
shoulder.

"Then I will be like my mother. Will you train me
to be a warrior?"

"That is not something that I can do. To be a
Nubian warrior you must be of Nubia."

"Shen is not of Nubia and he is a warrior."

"Shen came to our kingdom as a warrior. Now he
trains within the compound to maintain his skills."

"If I come to Nubia, then may I train to become a
warrior?"

"I will speak to the princess, now!" The loud
voice came into Kandake's rooms from the hallway. A
response followed in Shen's voice, but it was too low
for Kandake to understand what he said.

"I am Tjaty, advisor to Pharaoh of Egypt! I will
go where I please!"

"A dead man advises no one."

Kandake walked to the doorway to find out what
the commotion was about.

"You!" Herihor spat. "You dare to direct one of
Pharaoh's own guards? This is not Nubia. You have
no authority in this kingdom!"

Herihor appeared to be beside himself with rage. Kandake did not allow her own anger to enter. Everything Uncle Dakká had taught her about a warrior's need for control flooded through her.

"Tjaty Herihor, if you will tell me what your concern is, I am certain I can clarify the matter to your satisfaction."

He made to step through the doorway to enter her rooms. Shen stood before him preventing his forward progress. Herihor took a step backwards, appearing to collect himself.

"Princess Kandake, it appears you directed one of the pharaoh's guards to disobey the orders I gave him."

"I am not certain I understand what you are speaking of," Kandake said.

"I told him to prevent anyone touching the vessels of the pharaoh. Yet you instructed that he allow that child to handle them." He pointed to Naomi. "How dare you touch anything belonging to the pharaoh?"

With a backhanded sweep of her arm, Kandake nudged Naomi behind her. "She is a child. Do not frighten or threaten her. The guard is a man instructed by his ruler. If there is a problem you should take it up with Pharaoh Nakhtnebef. It was he who gave the child permission."

"Pharaoh?" Herihor glared at Kandake, but said nothing. After a time he said, "You dismissed the servants that were assigned to care for your needs. Instead you have chosen a child to attend you. I imagine children prefer the company of children." A nasty smirk crossed his face as he turned to leave.

36

The next morning Kandake rode out to where the Nubian warriors were encamped. As she arrived she caught sight of Prince Khabebesh sparring with Natasen. She dismounted and handed the reins to Shen.

"How long have they been working?" Kandake asked Soleb, the warrior nearest her.

"Quite some time, Princess Kandake," the warrior said, smirking. "Prince Natasen is every bit as exacting as Prince Dakká. He corrects the pharaoh's son's every move."

Kandake watched her brother as he required Khabebesh to repeat a particular thrust and pivot for the fifth time since her arrival. She felt compassion for the prince as his arms began to tremble with fatigue. "Prince Natasen, may I demonstrate?"

At Natasen's beckoning she stood before her brother and executed the move with meticulous precision. In doing so she was able to prevent Natasen's attack which forced him to abandon his offensive progress, driving him into a defensive position.

"May I observe that once more, Princess Kandake?" Khabebesh asked. "I fail to see how what you are doing is much different than my attempts."

"Of course, Prince," she said. "If Prince Natasen will allow it, I will move at a slower pace so that you can see our smaller movements as well."

"A slower pace will aid him," Natasen said. "Prince Khabebesh, please take particular note of what Princess Kandake does with her weapon hand in relation to the placement of her feet."

They executed the move again. Prince Khabebesh stepped as close to them as he dared. He even mirrored Kandake's movements with his own body.

"I see it!" His voice held the excitement of a child when spotting his first scape's nest in which the eggs are the same mottled color as the ground. "Her shield prevents and confuses her opponent in seeing the movement of her feet while her weapon nearly mirrors her steps but twists away at the last moment. "Please, may I try it again?"

Khabebesh's discovery renewed his energy. He repeated the action again and again until finally Natasen called an end to the practice. Even as Kandake visited with her brother, Prince Khabebesh removed himself to a corner of the camp where he could be seen practicing the move over and over again.

"He is like a child in his eagerness," Natasen said. "Khabebesh attacks every new skill with fervor."

"Alara says the same of him as they discuss the history of nearby kingdoms and their rulers," Kandake said. "This is not the disinterested, uninvolved person we found upon our arrival."

Natasen agreed with his sister and pointed out areas of improvement as he watched the pharaoh's son. "Have you spoken with Nakhtnebef about the stib?"

"I have, but I have yet to tell him we believe Tjaty to be at the root of it."

As they spoke, grit and sand was kicked into the air by the hooves of a hastily reined in horse. Tjaty Herihor jumped from his mount and strode to the brother and sister.

"I see that you are now interfering with the manner in which Egypt manages its warriors." The sweep of his hand indicated the Nubian camp.

"These are not Egypt's warriors," Natasen said. "These are Nubian citizens and warriors of Nubia." His voice held an edge that Kandake knew would be supported by her brother's blade and bow. She placed a discreet hand on his, a signal for him to hold back.

This man is provoking Natasen, why? What does he hope to gain? Kandake waited.

"You children," Herihor said, a sneer creeping over his face. "You believe you have power in a kingdom that is not your own. This is not Nubia, it is Egypt. And in Pharaoh's illness, I, Tjaty Herihor, am in control of this kingdom."

"Please forgive my ignorance, Tjaty," Kandake said. "But if Pharaoh Nakhtnebef is not well enough to rule, would not that duty fall to his son, Prince Khabebesh?"

"The prince is as much a child as you. Look at him." Herihor nodded his head in the direction of the corner where Khabebesh practiced. "He plays with weapons as a young boy plays with sticks in the dirt. It is a wonder he has not cut off his own arm." He turned toward Kandake. "And you, a little girl who thinks because she will one day be queen has the ability to rule. You are not fit to rule. You cannot tolerate the company of women so you replace them with another little girl."

The Nubian warriors standing within earshot came to the alert. They stood behind Herihor, glaring at his back with muscles tensed for action. A quick hand-signal from Kandake caused them to take a step backwards.

"They will do nothing," Herihor said. "They are under agreement to serve Egypt. I am Egypt!" He laughed and returned to his horse, mounted and rode away.

"I hate that man," Prince Khabebesh said. He moved to stand next to Kandake staring at Herihor's retreating form.

37

Kandake walked to the pharaoh's private courtyard to share evening meal with Nakhtnebef and Khabebesh. One long table was spread with a linen cloth before the pharaoh and his son. At the other end of the courtyard a similar table was set with varying platters of food, meats, cheeses, herbs, fruit, and bread. Several servants stood at the end of the food-laden table waiting to serve them.

Kandake's brothers, Alara and Natasen, joined her at the pharaoh's table. Naomi worked with Nakhtnebef's servants, washing the dishes before the food was served. Shen stood behind Kandake. Whenever she looked at him, his eyes were on Herihor as the advisor walked through the doorway. Shen's expression was one of adversary measuring his enemy.

"Tjaty," Nakhtnebef said as Herihor entered and took his place at the table. "I was just telling our

Nubian guests about the prince's plans for that fertile land along the Nile."

Herihor shook his head and smiled at no one in particular. "Pharaoh, these are the dreams of a child. That plot of land is not large enough to bear much food. It is a waste of time. The people he has living there would better serve the kingdom placed elsewhere. They are not farmers. They should be working making bricks to build the tomb that will honor your memory and serve as a suitable home in the afterlife."

"Tjaty, do not worry. It will be some time before I need that home. What I must know at this time is if Prince Khabebesh has the wisdom to rule Egypt after me. This project will tell me much."

"Great Pharaoh, your son has your blood and we will see his greatness as he gets older. What Egypt needs is the assurance that the kingdom will stand until that day comes."

Prince Khabebesh opened his mouth to comment. Kandake saw Alara give a tight shake of his head. The prince pressed his lips together but his expression told those observing that his silence would not last long.

"Yes, but to place one of Egypt's governor's upon the throne would not only cause the people to question the right of Prince Khabebesh to rule, there is no guarantee that upon the arrival of his maturity the governor would relinquish the throne."

"That is why wisdom would have you choose someone other than a governor."

"And who might that be?" Khabebesh asked. He looked from his father to Herihor, then back to his father again.

"Someone you trust," Herihor said. "Someone who has served the throne without question."

"I see the wisdom of that, Tjaty" Nakhtnebef said. "That would be important to do if I were of poor health."

"Great Pharaoh, you have been ill, of late. And our priests and healers have not been able to cure you. You lose strength by the day."

"That has been true, but I am feeling stronger today." Nakhtnebef sat taller in his seat.

"You have felt stronger before, Pharaoh, but each time the illness returns."

"The illness will not return, Princess Kandake promised," Naomi said looking from Kandake to the pharaoh.

"You dare speak in our presence!" Herihor roared at the young girl. "You are a servant and a child. You have no place here. Leave us!"

"I will leave, but she is not only a princess, she is the goddess, Sakhmet daughter of Ra!" Naomi folded her arms across her chest. "Tell him, Princess."

"What stories have you been telling this child?" Herihor demanded, rounding on Kandake.

"I have told her no such thing. In fact, I have assured her that I am not the goddess.

"She will tell you she is not, but we know that she is," Naomi said.

"What 'we' are you speaking of and what has you so convinced that you would dare speak in the presence of your Pharaoh." The smirk Herihor wore was humorless and filled with malice.

"The viper did not strike her. She fights against Pharaoh's warriors and triumphs. She was created from the desert sands of Egypt!"

Nakhtnebef leaned forward, listening in earnest to what Naomi was saying.

"These things mean nothing." Herihor spluttered. "Pharaoh, you cannot believe the tales carried by a child."

Naomi approached the pharaoh and bowed before him. "It is true! I did exactly what she told me and Pharaoh regained his strength!"

Gasps could be heard throughout the room. Those servants preparing the meal stood stock-still hanging on every word the young girl said. Herihor stared at Kandake, first with widened eyes, then contempt. The expression on Nakhtnebef's face was one of awe.

"Pharaoh, do not listen to this. These are simply tales shared between children. The princess is the daughter of King Amani of Nubia, nothing more."

"Can you speak for Ra?" Nakhtnebef said. "Are you now a priest?"

"No Great Pharaoh, I am only saying that if the princess is the goddess, why has she not told us who she is and her purpose for visiting us. Besides, none of the priests have informed us of a visitation."

"The priests would inform you of no such thing. Such tellings would come to me, I am Pharaoh!"

"Great Pharaoh, I am only saying—"

"Silence!" Nakhtnebef bellowed, interrupting him. "I would hear from the priests. We will have this matter settled this night."

"I will send for them Great Pharaoh Nakhtnebef, but the temples of Ra and Sakhmet are a day's ride from the city," Herihor dissembled. "You will have you answer, but not this night."

"Send to the temple of Ptah! He is the husband of Sakhmet. I am certain that the priests there would know their god's wife! We will not eat until we have heard from the priests of Ptah." Nakhtnebef pinned Naomi with a watchful glare. "Now tell me, young one, what else do you know of this princess?"

38

Kandake sat in disbelief watching and listening as Nakhtnebef and Herihor discussed whether she was the goddess Sakhmet or not. Naomi told in detail of how Kandake had caught the viper with her bare hands and that the snake did not even attempt to strike her. She told the pharaoh of how Kandake had protected her from the beatings from the other servants.

"The princes from Nubia bow to her and she drinks a lot of pomegranate juice, especially when she is angry." This last Naomi added as surety for convincing Nakhtnebef.

The pharaoh stared at Kandake. She held his gaze with her own. *Surely he does not believe what Naomi is saying.*

"Pharaoh Nakhtnebef, I am the daughter of King Amani of Nubia," Kandake said. "I fight because I am a warrior. I happen to enjoy the juice of pomegranates, but I especially enjoy brined olives and honeyed dates, as well. These cannot be the preferences of a goddess."

"What of your ability to know what ails me when my healers do not. And your ability to bring me lasting relief?" Nakhtnebef said. "I believe we must wait for the priests' decisions before we will know the truth."

The priests of Ptah came into the courtyard. They bowed before Nakhtnebef, but their eyes stayed on Kandake.

"How may we serve you?" The priest who addressed the pharaoh was taller than the other two. His skin was dark, kissed by the sun. It was almost the same rich brown as Kandake's. He wore a jeweled collar that was as opulent as that worn by Nakhtnebef. "Why have you called the servants of the great god Ptah?"

"I am told that this one of Nubia is the wife of our God," the pharaoh said. "She denies it but I am told things that cause me to doubt what she says. I need you to tell me what is truth."

"Who tells you such things about this one?" The priest rose and addressed Nakhtnebef, but his eyes never left Kandake.

"The child," the pharaoh said. His hand swept toward Naomi. "She insists that Princess Kandake is Sakhmet, daughter of Ra."

"Come to me, child," the priest said.

Naomi stood from her kneeling position and walked to stand before the priest.

"Tell me your name. Where are your parents?"

"I am Naomi. My mother and father have died, but I live in the palace serving Pharaoh."

"What gods do you serve?" The priest pinned Naomi with his gaze.

"I serve the god Ra, but I promised the princess that if she would heal our Pharaoh, I would make a pilgrimage to the temple of Sakhmet and leave an offering."

"Tell me what brings you to believe that this young woman is the goddess? Did she tell you that?"

"No, she tried to get me to believe that she is not, but I know better." Naomi went on to tell the priest all of the things that convinced her of Kandake's true identity. She left nothing out and even added a few instances she had not shared with Nakhtnebef.

The priest listened with grave attention. He asked for clarification on a few points, but each time bade Naomi to continue. When the young girl had finished, the priest directed his attention back toward Kandake. His gaze was unwavering.

"Come to me," he called to Kandake.

Though his voice was compelling, Kandake stayed in her seat.

"Come to me," he beckoned again.

Kandake did not move.

"I command you to come to me," the priest beckoned a third time.

"Please forgive the offense of my seat," Kandake said. "But I am not of the habit of obeying any command other than my king's."

"Do you serve the god Ra?" he asked.

"I must say that Ra is not the god of Nubia."

"You appear to be of the age a girl attains womanhood in your kingdom. Have you taken a husband?"

"No, I am a warrior first and choose to focus on my skill before I take a husband." *Why is he asking me these things?*

"Is it true that you will rule Nubia following King Amani and still you have not taken a husband?" The priest's gaze became more intense as he waited for her answer.

"It is true that I will rule, but I need no husband to direct my kingdom. The husband I choose will be one who understands my strength and respects my wisdom and skill as a warrior. Nubia will look to me for direction and will expect me to lead them. The husband I choose already understands this and is confident in my power. *I may not be ready to choose, but I now understand who my choice must be.*

As if reading her thoughts, the priest smiled and shifted his focus back to Nakhtnebef.

"Pharaoh Nakhtnebef," the priest said. "I have come to a decision."

The pharaoh gave the priest his complete attention. Herihor sat back in his seat and awaited the priest's answer.

"The strength and spirit of Ra and Sakhmet rest deep within this one. I can feel their presence inside her. If she is not our goddess, I am certain she is guided by her."

"How can you say such things?" Herihor demanded. The words flew from his mouth. "She is not of Egypt. She has even told you that she does not worship our gods."

"What gods do you serve that you would argue with the servant of Ptah?" the priest asked, his anger evident.

"Thank you for your understanding," Nakhtnebef said to the priest. "Please receive my offering." He directed one of the servants to give the priest a small casket of gold and jewels. The priests turned toward Kandake and executed a deep bow before they took their leave.

"Great Pharaoh, you cannot believe that this child is the goddess incarnate?" Herihor said.

"Tjaty, you have served me well, but you test the lengths of my tolerance. Arguing with the priests, that is no way to represent this throne!"

"I meant no offense, Great Pharaoh, but this one," Herihor pointed toward Kandake, "has unduly influenced those around the throne. Had it not been for the strain of your illness, you would see this for yourself."

"Tjaty, I have not been more invigorated. Yet it appears that you must be suffering from the weight of responsibilities my illness has placed upon you. I release you to take your day's rest."

The eyes bulged from Herihor's sockets. His rage purpled his face. He slammed his jaw closed with such a snap, Kandake heard the meeting of his teeth and wondered if any had been broken. Herihor marched from the room with tight, measured strides.

"We must excuse Tjaty Herihor. My illness has placed greater stress upon him than he is accustomed to bearing," the pharaoh said. "When the gods appoint one to rule such a kingdom as Egypt, the weight he carries is supported by the gods themselves. When a man attempts to bear this burden without their assistance…. You can see for yourself the effect of that strain.

Kandake's gaze followed the back of Herihor as he left the courtyard.

What I see Pharaoh, are the effects of rage. Herihor behaves as a man who has lost a battle and I am certain he does not intend to lose a war. I will be watching that one.

39

Kandake had returned to her rooms to prepare for the night. Natasen appeared at her doorway and requested entrance. As he came in, Alara was close on his heels.

"I am concerned that Herihor will become more dangerous after this," Natasen said. "He does not appear to be a man that surrenders his plans."

"No he does not," Kandake said. She directed Naomi to go to bed.

"Are you angry with me, princess?" Naomi asked. "I had to tell the priests the truth. To lie to them would mean punishment in the afterlife."

'I am not angry with you. You told them what you believe to be truth." Kandake laid a gentle hand upon Naomi's shoulder. "You must rest now, tomorrow promises to be a very busy day."

Naomi left them to go to her sleeping area while the others continued their discussion in their Nubian tongue.

"What do you think Herihor will do?" Kandake asked Alara. "I am certain he is planning something."

"He cannot afford not to. Now that the priests have all but declared you to be their goddess, he must do something to dispel that notion or rid Egypt of your presence."

"I will not allow that to happen," Shen said. "I have pledged my protection to the future of Nubia. I will not fail her queen."

"Thank you, Shen," Kandake said. "I trust your skills, but we must also think of Egypt's throne. Herihor means to have it. I do not believe he is strong enough to take it by force, but if something were to happen to the pharaoh, he could claim it by declaring Khabebesh unfit to rule. To carry out that plan, he must attack Nakhtnebef."

"Then we must protect Nakhtnebef and at the same time insure that he sees the prince's true abilities." Alara said.

"I can put together a strategy that will secure the pharaoh's safety whenever he is outside the palace." Natasen gave his head a strong nod accentuating his ability.

"And I can continue to encourage the prince in how he presents himself to Nakhtnebef and the governors," Alara added.

"That leaves the pharaoh's safety inside the palace to me," Kandake said. "Having the priests confidence in me and Nakhtnebef's confidence in his priests, I should be able to convince him that he is in danger and allow me to help."

"I will assist the princess," Shen said. "I have spoken with the remaining Scythian warriors and it appears as I have believed. Aside from those we encountered in the desert, they remain faithful to the Sovereign." He shifted his weight and folded his arms across his chest. "They feared Kuska's skill as an assassin and believed they would never return to our kingdom. They chose to serve the pharaoh and await an occasion such as this to prove their loyalty to the Sovereign. With Kuska imprisoned, they no longer fear him and are eager for a task that will demonstrate their allegiance."

"What if they are deceiving you?" Alara asked

"This band I wear represents my ranking in the army of the Sovereign." Shen held up his arm displaying the symbol. "It grants me the power to execute them in his name. This they understand, as well."

The party from Nubia discussed their plans well into the night. When they had finished, each was certain of their part and how to use their particular skills to save Pharaoh Nakhtnebef and expose Herihor.

૭૦ ૨૭

"Good morning," Kandake said as she entered the pharaoh's courtyard. He and Khabebesh appeared to be in deep discussion as they ate their morning meal.

"Good morning, Princess," Pharaoh said. "The prince and I were just discussing the situation with the warriors of Nubia. He believes that we are no longer in need of their services." Nakhtnebef invited Kandake to sit with them and instructed the servants to bring her a plate of food. Kandake noted that each dish was washed in clear, clean water before any food was placed upon it.

I see that Nakhtnebef is taking our conversation in earnest. She smiled to herself as she accepted the plate of food.

"While Nubia is willing to assist Egypt in maintaining its strength, it brings the kingdom greater joy knowing that our ally and neighbor can stand in power." She took a bite of the meat and cheese she had been served. A drinking bowl was placed before her. It was filled with pomegranate juice. *He has also taken to heart the words of the priests.* She sipped and enjoyed the flavor.

"Thank you, Princess Kandake," he said. "Please extend my gratitude to King Amani when you return. I am drafting the order releasing your warriors from my service. They will be able to return to Nubia with you." He put the last flourishes to the document he inscribed and added his seal to it.

"My apologies, Great Pharaoh," Herihor said as he entered the courtyard. "I left orders with the servants to rouse me the moment you stirred, but they did not do so."

"No apologies needed," Nakhtnebef said. "I instructed the servants to allow you to sleep. You have been serving the throne with such diligence during my illness that I fear it has weighted you with great strain.

I realized the injustice I had done you the moment you questioned the priests of Ptah."

Herihor came to an abrupt stop as he took in the presence of Kandake sitting at the table with the pharaoh and Khabebesh.

"Would you care to share morning meal with us?" Nakhtnebef asked his advisor. He indicated the empty chair next to him and signaled the servants to bring him food. "I was just explaining to Princess Kandake that Egypt no longer requires the services of Nubian warriors. In fact I have drawn up the decree just this moment." He passed a rolled hide fixed with the pharaoh's seal to a messenger to be taken to Natasen in the warrior camps.

"Pharaoh Nakhtnebef, I am not certain that is the best thing to do at this time. Egypt has just come out of war with Assyria and their spies and warriors may still be lurking within our lands."

"I do not believe that to be so, but if it is, Prince Khabebesh assures me that our warriors are more than able to protect this kingdom."

"You would listen to the advice of the prince?" Herihor sputtered. "I am advisor to the throne of Egypt. Pharaoh you would do well to hear my words."

"Our warriors are well trained," Khabebesh said. "It would serve to build the people's confidence in them, as well as the throne, to see the Nubian warriors leave and our men protecting the kingdom once more."

"Whose counsel have you been listening to?" Herihor's accusing stare rested upon Kandake. "I am the advisor of Egypt! You should be listening to me!"

"You are my father's advisor," Khabebesh said, his voice calm and infused with strength and authority. "Your position will end at the close of his reign."

40

Kandake watched as Herihor's expression shifted from shock to anger and finally to determination.

"I am Pharaoh Nakhtnebef's advisor and I have served him well. It is your youth and inexperience that allows you to speak before weighing the consequences of your declarations." Herihor swung his attention to Kandake and spewed his venom in her direction. "In Nubia children are allowed to run before they learn to walk. Even their women grasp at roles that are better left to men."

Herihor stood and gathered his robes about him. "Princess, please enlighten me. Is it that the men of Nubia are so weak of mind that their women can lead them by the nose like cows fixed in mud? Or is it that the women of that kingdom are so hardened that your men have thought surrender more promising? I have been told that there is more warmth in the embrace of a granite obelisk than there is in the arms of a Nubian woman." He strode from the table to leave the courtyard. As he approached the doorway he turned to face the pharaoh. His countenance had taken on the glow of triumph which he enhanced with a nasty sneer.

"It is a good thing you have released the Nubians from our service. I would have used them to secure what is mine, but in the end they would have proved too costly to the throne and their ways may have contaminated the things of Egypt."

"The man has gone mad!" Nakhtnebef said. "The responsibilities he has taken on have proven to be more than he can carry."

"I do not believe that to be the case, Pharaoh Nakhtnebef," Kandake said watching the back of Herihor disappear through the doorway. "I believe it is evil that has consumed him. He is a dangerous man that has gone to complete some foul task."

She looked about the room. Spotting Naomi, she beckoned the girl to her. "Pharaoh Nakhtnebef, I do not trust this man. I am certain he plans destruction to the throne of Egypt. Allow me to send word to my brother, Natasen, that he may come with enough warriors to ensure the protection of the pharaoh and the prince."

"Tjaty is angry, but his devotion to Egypt would prevent him bringing harm to the kingdom."

"I would not name him as an assassin before, but I am certain that he is the one that directs Chatha's hand in causing your illness." Kandake leveled her gaze to capture the pharaoh's and locked it there. "Chatha was a member of your personal guard."

"Great Pharaoh," Khabebesh said. "I must agree with Princess Kandake. I have never trusted Tjaty. He poisons your mind about my abilities. I have worked hard to know the people of Egypt and love them all. I have studied the history of this kingdom and understand the things that make her great. I have even examined the flow and profit of our trade.

"Tjaty is aware of all of this. You send him to teach me the things I need to know to rule. Instead, he speaks with me about matters of the kitchen and takes me to catch fish. He does not tell you what I have learned. He tells you that I am young and must be given time to mature." The prince planted both hands upon the table and leaned toward his father.

"I watch your health fail and study with increased fervor, fearing that my time to rule this kingdom will come much sooner than it should. It was not until Prince Alara arrived that my study has been noticed or appreciated. He asks questions that cause me to think, teaches me the value of a true advisor, he even encouraged my study of the use of weapons. This man you call Tjaty is evil and your death would bring him great pleasure!"

Pharaoh Nakhtnebef shook his head in sadness. "I have not ruled this kingdom as I should. My son will serve Egypt better." He sagged against the back of his chair, discouragement written in every line of his bearing. "Princess Kandake, the throne of Egypt once again accepts the aid of Nubia."

Kandake scribbled a message upon a small scrap of hide and instructed Naomi to deliver it to Natasen. "After you deliver this," she said, "you are to remain within the Nubian camp until I come for you." Wide-eyed, Naomi nodded her head in agreement. As she left the courtyard going through the kitchens, Herihor walked through the doorway. He leaned against the wall as one who takes his ease while waiting for a friend on a pleasant evening.

"Tjaty," Pharaoh said. "Have you come to discuss your insulting behavior and seek the forgiveness of the throne?"

"Not at all, I have come to watch the look upon your face as you see your reign come to an end."

41

"You have truly gone mad!" Nakhtnebef shouted. "Take this man to see the healer. Bind him if you must."

No one moved. Herihor's sneer grew into a grin.

Kandake looked about the room. *I do not like this. The man looks too confident.*

"Pentu! I am speaking to you," the pharaoh said. "Remove Tjaty from my sight."

Still no one moved. Herihor began to laugh—a sound that contained no humor.

Confusion clouded Nakhtnebef's countenance. Realization supplanted confusion, moving across his face as a gradual wave of awareness came upon him.

"You see it do you not, the end of your reign? This is beyond value!" Herihor seemed beside himself with pleasure. "Pentu, remove the servants to the kitchens. Senebi, go with him. Keep them there. They are to speak with no one. Should they try to escape…I do not need to tell you how to handle that."

"If you continue, you will only succeed in securing your own death," Nakhtnebef said.

Herihor released another bark of humorless laughter. He turned his attention back toward the pharaoh.

"Pharaoh…I will call you that for now," Herihor said. "These are the last moments of your reign. Enjoy of them what you can. The remainder of my guard will arrive before long and when they do you will no longer rule Egypt." He continued to speak as he walked toward the table.

Kandake caught sight of a shadow near the doorway. She used every bit of discipline to keep her gaze away from that direction. She stole a final glance, hoping that Natasen had received her message.

"There is no need for you to keep watch upon the door, Princess. There is no help coming for you. Prince Natasen is out at the warrior camps and my men are searching for Prince Alara."

"You would do well to end this, now," Kandake said. "Should harm come to anyone of Nubia there is no stone that will hide you, no wall that will protect you. Our warriors will find you and deliver the punishment you have worked so hard to earn."

"That would be a problem if I were not going to be the next pharaoh of Egypt before the sun leaves the sky," Herihor said, gloating. "I have no intention of harm toward any of you, except perhaps the current pharaoh. Once I have taken the throne, King Amani will not dare strike back. How would he explain going to war over a problem that exists solely within the government of another kingdom. But then you are only a child, and these are things for men to deliberate." He lifted the pharaoh's vessel and drank from it.

Rage flowed through Kandake like water through the Nile. She found herself taking deep breaths and expelling them at a slow, deliberate pace. *You have defiled the trust that lies between Egypt and Nubia. I vow that this act will not go unanswered.*

"Tjaty Herihor," an Egyptian warrior said. "We found this prince lurking at the doorway. It took some convincing to get him to come inside." Two other Egyptian warriors dragged a struggling Alara between them.

Kandake's heart was stuck a blow. She had hoped Alara would not be caught up in this, but here he was in Herihor's grasp.

"Release him," Herihor barked. "This is the son of the king of Nubia. We do not wish to begin our relationship with that kingdom explaining why the responsibility of his children's injuries should not be laid at our feet."

"Yes, Tjaty Herihor." The warriors released him, but one of the them plowed an elbow into Alara's mid-section. The blow left Alara doubled over and down on one knee wheezing for breath.

Kandake's eyes burned with fury witnessing the mistreatment of her brother. *I will repay your cruelty. My brother is no warrior. There is no justification for your actions.*

"That is not what I commanded," Herihor bellowed. "If you cannot follow an order maybe your next duty will be protecting Pharaoh Nakhtnebef in the afterlife. Help him to rise!"

The Egyptian warrior stepped in front of Alara, took hold of his shoulders and lifted him to his feet. Alara took one step forward bringing his arm up, gripping his wrist as he rose. He shifted his weight, twisted at his waist, and brought his shoulder forward with power, delivering his own elbow strike to the warrior's face. The bone of Alara's arm connected with the bone of the man's cheek. Caught by surprise, the warrior went down with a thud. Blood ran from a cut just below his eye.

Kandake cheered. Those warriors acting as guard snickered. The downed warrior scrambled to his feet to answer Alara's punch with a few of his own.

"That will be enough!" Herihor roared. "Prince, I would not suggest you attempt anything like that again. Princess, do not encourage your brother in further incidents. My men fail to have the discipline one would expect of them. I cannot be responsible for their actions should you provide them additional provocation."

The pharaoh's personal guard filed into the courtyard—the entire unit. Kandake watched as they lined up before Herihor, each of them avoided eye contact with either Nakhtnebef or the prince.

"You left the selection of your personal guard to me," Herihor goaded the pharaoh. "Did you truly believe I would select men who were loyal to you?"

Kandake searched the face of each man in the lineup. She discovered that three of the men were Scythian. She turned to look at Shen. He gave her a single tight bob of his head. She hoped he meant that these were the men who Shen said were loyal to their Scythian ruler.

Chaos broke out within the kitchens. Servants were shrieking and dishes were crashing to the floor. Then there was silence.

"It appears we have fewer servants to provide our meals," Herihor said, but the joke provided no humor for Kandake.

I will add their lives to the list of those for which I will charge you. When it comes time for you to pay, Tjaty, I trust you will find that humorous as well.

42

Kandake stared at Herihor. Her hands ached to hold her bow. She watched the advisor revel in his accomplishments.

"Princess," Herihor directed his attention toward Kandake. "Your expression tells me that you do not approve of my actions. Do not trouble yourself. Egypt will continue its relations with Nubia, but there will be a few changes. If King Amani wishes the safe return of his precious heir, he will agree to the conditions set by the new pharaoh."

Rage struck Kandake and coursed through her as the force of lightning through a dry stump. Her bones vibrated with the emotion. The muscles in her body burned with fury. She was nearly consumed with it. She had been angry before, but nothing like this. Outrage combined with betrayal stitched together with the thread of retribution boiled within her and she hoped her arrow would be the needle that guided it toward its mark.

She took a step toward the former advisor.

"I can read your thoughts, Princess. You may be able to harm me, but before that could happen you would have to fight your way beyond the men I have hand-picked to serve me, all of them warriors of Egypt."

If you could read my thoughts, you would know that I will stop you. I am returning to Nubia and nothing you do, or direct, will prevent me. What I promise is that when I do, you will not be seated upon Egypt's throne.

A shadow in the doorway to the kitchens caught her attention. A hand flashed her a signal.

Kandake took another step forward.

"I must insist that you remain where you are," Herihor told her. "The knife you wear is not enough to protect you from these men." He nodded in the direction of his guard. "Remove that before she is harmed."

Two of the Egyptian warriors advanced on Kandake. She unsheathed her blade and assumed a defensive posture. They continued to come in her direction. Kandake sprinted to meet them head on. She kicked the first man with the flat of her foot to his middle and swiped the edge of her knife down the thigh of the second.

Shen ran forward and plowed into the first row of the guard. Nubian warriors streamed from the kitchen doorway and engaged them from the rear. The mob of warriors in combat filled the courtyard with the sounds of flesh striking flesh, the clang and clamor of blade upon blade. Cries of agony echoed from the walls as fighters were struck down.

Kandake fought with every bit of skill taught by her uncle. The man facing her misjudged her strength and intent. He struck her middle with a powerful fist. His face reported his shock when Kandake failed to succumb to the strike. She utilized his momentary distraction and struck his temple with the hilt of her knife. His dazed condition made it that much easier for Kandake to knock him to the ground.

The battle was even, for every traitorous guard that fell to injury or death, a Nubian warrior fell. Kandake fought hand-to-knife and knife-to-hand striving to keep the advisor or one of his men away from Nakhtnebef. Khabebesh fought at her side. Alara brawled and struggled against the betrayers as well, but he was no match for men who had trained and battled all of their lives.

He fell to the ground. Blood ran from the wound in his side. Kandake could not get to him. The warrior she contended with would not go down. She needed to get to Alara. The blood coming from his injury had begun to pool on the flagstone beneath him. He needed the medicines she wore in the pouch hanging from her waist.

Kandake pounded the warrior before her. He answered her every strike. She executed a sweep to his feet, but the man she fought hopped and maintained his balance. Kandake glanced again at Alara and the warrior's knife sliced into her thigh. The pain brought back her focus, but she was beginning to tire.

My brother will not die! My father will not lose his children! Determination fed her the energy she needed.

The warrior she fought raised his arm to deliver a chopping blow to her shoulder. Instead of stepping to the side to dodge it, Kandake stepped into him and toward the striking arm. She brought her blade up as she pivoted away and plunged it into his back with a backward swing of her arm. The strike lacked the force to deliver a mortal wound, but it was enough to send the man to the ground.

Kandake dashed to her brother's side. She laid her hand upon his chest and was rewarded with the rise and fall of his breath and the even thump of his heart. She ripped the fabric of his garment to give her a clear view of the wound and used the dry, unstained edges to wipe away the oozing blood. The gash was long, but not deep. Alara would not die from the slice in his flesh.

She poured the contents of her pouch on the ground beside him and found the packet that contained the salve she needed. It was a mixture of frankincense, vegetable fat, and herbs. Kandake packed the gash in his side with it. She then tied a strip of his garment over the wound.

From her place next to Alara, Kandake surveyed the battle. Every warrior within the courtyard battled for his life. She took note of the warriors of Nubia that had entered from the kitchen, she saw the Scythians that now chose to fight alongside Shen against the Egyptian guard. She saw everyone but Herihor. Kandake scoured the room, but he was not there—nor was Nakhtnebef. Khabebesh was missing as well. Kandake pushed up from the floor. She scooped the salves, herbs, and other medicines back into the healer's pouch, picked up her knife and ran in search of those missing three.

Kandake stepped into the throne room. It was empty save for a few servants tending the care of furniture and floor. When they spotted her, as a group, they pointed toward a passageway behind the throne. She assumed they indicated the direction the pharaoh and Herihor had gone.

She tore through the doorway and down the corridor, uncertain of where it led. The hallway was not well lit, since there were no windows to the outside and only one lit torch. She slowed her pace as she came upon the first of five closed doors. She pressed her ear to it, listening for any clue to the location of the now captured ruler.

No sound came to her from inside. Kandake nudged the door. It opened the breadth of two fingers. Applying her ear to the space, she listened again. Hearing no sound, she swung the door open to its fullest. The empty space urged her on to the next closed entryway.

The door opened as she approached it. Kandake lowered herself to a defensive posture and shifted her weight to the balls of her feet. The hilt of her knife was a comforting weight to her hand. She raised her arm, prepared to strike. The man exiting the room was not Herihor, neither did he wear the trappings of an Egyptian warrior. As more of him backed through the doorway, Kandake spotted the collar that identified the man as a palace servant.

She grabbed his arm and pinned him against the wall. Kandake held him captive with her forearm pressed into the man's throat and her knee adding pressure to a most vulnerable area. The man stared back at her in wide-eyed terror. Kandake placed her lips against his ear.

"Is Pharaoh Nakhtnebef in that room," she whispered. The man said nothing. Kandake gave more force to the knee and accompanied it with the point of her blade to his side. The servant held his tongue, reluctant to speak until the tip of her knife pricked his flesh.

"Yes, Tjaty Herihor is inside with Pharaoh," the man said in a rasp. "Tjaty has said that I am to bring him a scribe. Pharaoh has something important that must be recorded."

43

Kandake's thoughts raced as she held the servant against the wall. *This must end! Herihor must be stopped!* Shadows of a plan streamed into her mind.

"Do as you have been instructed. You send the scribe, but have him report to me," she said. She released the servant. His eyes widened even more as she removed her blade from his side. "You tell the scribe to report to me. Pharaoh Nakhtnebef is in danger." The man scampered away like a hen avoiding a jackal.

Kandake edged as close to the doorway as she dared. Mumbled voices came through the opening. She strained to hear the conversation.

"I told you to sit, Prince. No harm will come to your beloved father as long as you both do as I command."

Herihor's voice came to her through the gap. It put her in mind of a hyena. This man was on the scent of his prey and there would be nothing to divert him regardless of what he promised.

He will kill them both. Kandake heard the scuffing of sandals coming down the corridor. She moved away from the door to meet the scribe.

"I have been summoned," the man said. He gave Kandake a quizzical look then riveted his gaze to the knife she held.

"Your pharaoh is in danger," she said, trying to gain his full attention. "Tjaty Herihor is ill and has gone mad. He believes if he kills the pharaoh and the prince he can rule this kingdom. You must do what I tell you or he may kill you as well."

The scribe's jaw dropped and he took two steps backward. His eyes darted this way and that as if looking for a way of escape.

"There is no way to get out of this unless you do exactly as I say," Kandake said. "If you do not obey my every word, Pharaoh Nakhtnebef and the prince will die. Tjaty Herihor will kill you as well."

The scribe opened his mouth to argue and took another step backward.

"I am Princess Kandake, future queen of Nubia," she said, packing all of the authority she had ever heard her father use into her voice. "You will assist me in saving your pharaoh or you will die here, by my hand."

The man froze. His jaw snapped shut. He gave the appearance of a trapped animal that accepts that his death is imminent. Every muscle in his body relaxed and his eyes lost the light of hope.

Kandake explained what she wanted him to do. She had him repeat her instructions and when he seemed certain of his task, she sent him into the room. He left the door ajar as she had told him.

Kandake waited in the corridor, listening. When Herihor's attention was absorbed in his instructions to the scribe, she walked in.

"Good afternoon, Princess," Herihor said. "I had hoped you would be detained in the courtyard until we had completed our work."

Kandake's gaze swept the room taking in every detail. Herihor kept Nakhtnebef within his grasp—one hand on the pharaoh's shoulder, the other hand held a blade to his throat. Prince Khabebesh stood several arm-lengths from the advisor, threatening him with a long-knife. The scribe sat at a table nearest the door. He arranged and rearranged an assortment of reed pens and sheets of papyrus, delaying the recording as she had instructed. He also left his pot of ink uncovered as they had discussed.

"This is not wise," Kandake said. "Whatever you are planning will not work."

"Of course it will. Pharaoh has been ill for some time. The prince is young and has not reached the age at which he is prepared to rule." Herihor forced Nakhtnebef to move with him taking a step away from Kandake. "As any responsible ruler, our Pharaoh is insuring that the kingdom will remain strong. It is his decree, that should he fall victim to his illness, I, Tjaty Herihor, should rule in his place until which time I deem his son fit to take the throne."

"There is no one that will believe you," the prince spat.

"It is not necessary that any believe me," Herihor said. "That is the reason for the scribe. He writes what the pharaoh dictates and the pharaoh will dictate." He added enough pressure to the knife he held at Nakhtnebef's throat that a thin line of the ruler's blood appeared. "And what the pharaoh says is law."

Herihor laughed. The sound he produced was devoid of mirth. It gave the impression of dried reeds rubbing against more dried reeds in a strong wind.

"I will not let you do it!" Prince Khabebesh edged toward the advisor, his blade held out in a menacing fashion.

"You cannot stop me." Herihor pressed in on the knife causing Nakhtnebef to yelp. "Scribe, ready yourself! Cease your fumbling! Pharaoh Nakhtnebef has something important to say." The scribe looked to Kandake. "Do not look to her, I have told you what to do!"

Kandake nodded for the scribe to do as Herihor said.

"Why does this man look to a child for permission?" The advisor sneered at the man sitting at the table. Then he turned to Kandake. "Nothing concerns you here, this is Egypt. Return to Nubia. I will send word to King Amani of the new Pharaoh seated upon Egypt's throne and that Nubia must set new accords with me!"

44

"The ally Nubia recognizes is Pharaoh Nakhtnebef," Kandake said. "You will not be known to King Amani, you have no throne!"

Khabebesh moved forward.

"Be still Prince! Another step and your father will join the gods!" Herihor switched his attention back to Kandake. "I have said for you to leave! There is nothing here for Nubia!"

"Egypt's throne has been threatened; Nubia does not abandon its allies!"

"Scribe!" Herihor bellowed. "Write what I tell you!"

The seated man lifted a reed pen. He reached to dip it into his inkpot. His hand shook and trembled. His left hand grappled the wrist of his right to steady it. The movement jostled the pot. It skittered toward the edge of the table and over it, sending it crashing to the floor.

Startled, the scribe shot to his feet upending the table. Papyrus sheets cascaded to the stone tile below. "I need more ink!" His voice pierced the air like that of a strangled hen as he scuttled backward toward the door and made his escape.

In the confusion, Prince Khabebesh charged Herihor. Kandake made use of the advisor's distraction. She took a running leap and slid feet-first into those of Nakhtnebef. She toppled the ruler, knocking him from Herihor's grasp.

Khabebesh clashed into Herihor. The two men fought, wielding their weapons. As iron struck against iron sparks flew from their weapons. Kandake helped Nakhtnebef to stand. She ripped a strip of fabric from her skirt and used it to bandage the cut at his neck.

Herihor advanced upon Khabebesh, swinging his long-knife, seeking an opening through which to plunge into the prince's flesh. Khabebesh's blade answered every strike. The look of fury he wore appeared to fuel his arm and the skill he used within the struggle. Back and forth their blades flew, colliding and clashing. The two battled—weapons flashing and hands grappling. The prince's foot settled upon a stray sheet of papyrus. It slid from under him. They crashed to the floor. The prince's head struck the heavy leg of a nearby bench. His form went still. Khabebesh lay unconscious.

Herihor rolled from atop the prince. As he stood, he leered at Kandake. "I told you to leave this kingdom. You did not. Instead, you chose to interfere with the affairs of Egypt." He moved in her direction.

In ministering to the wound on the pharaoh's neck, Kandake left her long-knife on the floor. She bent to reach for it. Herihor grabbed her about the waist and kicked the blade outside her grasp.

The door to the chamber flew open. Natasen and Shen burst into the room. Herihor wrenched Kandake against himself and held her there as a shield blocking the on-coming attackers.

The arms and chests of Natasen and Shen were slick with sweat. Blood smeared their garments—evidence to the battle they had just fought. They glared at the advisor holding Kandake pinned to himself.

"You would do well to release Princess Kandake," Alara said, coming into the room holding the wound in his side. "Your actions have placed the possibility of your greeting the morning's sun in great jeopardy." He moved toward the advisor. His voice had taken on the quality of cold, sharpened iron, a blade whose edge has been hammered into strength.

"The only thing that is in jeopardy at this time is the future of Nubia!" Herihor pulled the hand that was not holding Kandake from behind him. Within it he held the knife he'd used to fight Khabebesh. He placed it against her throat. "I will drag this blade across her neck with no more care than I would of dragging a carcass across the desert."

Alara stopped walking. His face fused into an expression of fury.

"Do not listen to him," Nakhtnebef said. "He will kill her just as he has done the prince."

"He is not dead," Herihor said, "but he will be after I have completed this transaction with our neighboring kingdom."

"Kill him!" the pharaoh yelled. "Bleed the pig!"

As they were talking, Kandake slipped her hand within the folds of her skirt and unsheathed the small dagger she wore next to her skin. In a stream of motion, Kandake struck. She plunged the dagger deep into the flesh of Herihor's thigh. The shock of her action caused the advisor to remove his blade from her throat and his arm loosened its grip about her waist.

Kandake spun away from the man. His blade-hand flashed to strike her. She blocked it with a lifted forearm. The defensive move protected her aimed-for neck, but resulted in a gash in her arm. The pain drove her to place her foot soundly and make her pivot smooth and accurate. Her answering strike sliced her knife's blade through the pulsing vein in his throat.

Herihor clutched his neck, but it did not stem the flow of life leaving him. Loathing filled his countenance as his body folded to the floor. His mouth worked, opening and closing like a fish pulled from the Nile. His face held the expression of the terrified.

"Sakhmet." The word came out in a hoarse whisper as his spirit left him.

.

45

Natasen, Shen, and Alara gathered staring at the now lifeless form of Herihor, former adviser to Pharaoh Nakhtnebef. Kandake joined the ruler as he attended to his unconscious son.

"He breathes!" Nakhtnebef said, relief flooding his voice. "My son lives!" He cradled the prince's head upon his lap. "If the jackal were not already dead, I would kill him myself."

"He will see how treachery is rewarded in the afterlife," Kandake said. She gave Herihor one last glance over her shoulder. "Please allow us to take Prince Khabebesh to his bed to rest."

"Yes, that would be wise." Nakhtnebef moved away so that his son could be lifted.

As Shen and Natasen began raising the prince, his eyes blinked several times before remaining open.

"Where is my father?" Khabebesh demanded, twisting and struggling to break free of those holding him. He gained his feet while scanning every portion of the chamber. Panic inscribed itself across his features until he caught sight of Nakhtnebef standing behind him. The two embraced thumping each other's backs with hardy blows.

"Where is Tjaty?" the prince asked. His father pointed to where he lay. Khabebesh walked to the spot and bent to examine the body. "Who did this?"

The room remained silent. No one volunteered the information. The prince searched the faces around him. Finally, Kandake stepped forward.

"I am the one," she said. Her voice came in hushed tones, her face devoid of emotion. "It is not a thing that brings me pride. There is no strength in taking the life of another, rather it speaks of weakness. I wish there had been another choice."

"But this man was evil," Khabebesh insisted. "He planned to kill Pharaoh. I believe he would have killed me, as well"

"I believe that, as well," she said, "but taking his life is not a choice that brings me pleasure"

"You are a warrior. Taking lives is what a warrior does!"

"That is where you are wrong, Prince. Protecting lives is what a warrior does." Kandake cleaned and replaced the small knife she wore against her skin. "A warrior that is strong never takes a life if there is another choice."

Prince Khabebesh shook his head as if in disbelief. He looked to the faces of Natasen and Shen, those he respected as seasoned warriors. The expressions he scanned were of stone.

"What the princess tells you is correct" Alara said. "Nubian warriors are known for many things—the accuracy of the bow, whether on foot or the back of a horse, their determination in battle, but most of all they are known for their strength. This comes from their respect for the lives of others."

Khabebesh looked from Alara to his father, then to Kandake, and finally back to Alara where he fastened his gaze for some time. At last he gave his head a concluding nod.

"What of the battle in my courtyard?" Nakhtnebef asked in the silence.

"It has ended," Natasen said. "Many of the men who had followed Herihor lay dead. The others are injured or subdued. They await your judgment."

Servants were called. Several of them lifted and removed the advisor's body, others set about restoring order to the room.

"Yes," Nakhtnebef said. His eyes trailed the body as it was moved past him. "We must set to right this evil that has been attempted and return Egypt to the joy the gods intended.

46

Pharaoh Nakhtnebef had declared that evening meal would be a feast to celebrate the successful visit and forthcoming departure of the representatives of Egypt's ally. Kandake returned to her rooms to prepare. She stepped into the cleansing booth to undress for her bath. Her entrance interrupted a heated conversation among the original women assigned to serve her with Naomi leading the argument.

"The duty is mine! I will see to the princess' bath." The young girl stood at the center of the ring of women.

"You have been called to assist with Pharaoh's meal. You must go to the kitchens," a servant said. "I will see to her bath."

Is not she the woman who feared to touch my breastplate? Now she is arguing for the opportunity to assist my bath. What has changed her?

"What is this discussion?" Kandake asked. She looked from face to face, but no one spoke.

"Princess, they say that I must leave you to work in the kitchens," Naomi said. "Have I done something to displease you?"

"She is not being punished, Princess," another of the women said. "She is being honored. Pharaoh Nakhtnebef has appointed Naomi to oversee his personal service. He is to eat nothing without her personal observation and approval."

"Princess, please do not send me away." Naomi looked at Kandake with pleading eyes.

Kandake brought Naomi to a nearby bench and sat the young girl down with her. "To serve the pharaoh in this fashion is truly an honor," she said. The words did not change Naomi's expression.

Kandake placed her hand beneath the girl's chin and lifted it. "Did not you tell me that you desire to train as a warrior and to become the pharaoh's protector?"

"Yes," Naomi said. The reluctance in her voice was plain for all to hear.

"An honor such as this can surely lead to a position as trusted as protector. And is this not another way of protecting your pharaoh?" Kandake saw interest and hope enter the young girl's eyes.

"Do you believe so, Princess?" Naomi said. "That is what I desire, to become Pharaoh's protector, like my mother had been."

"You have some time yet. You must train very hard and develop strong discipline."

"But my mother trained in Nubia. There is no training for a girl in this kingdom." Naomi's face was once again downcast.

"It may be possible that if you serve your pharaoh well, and prove that you are worthy of his trust, he may allow you to journey to Nubia to train with our warriors to develop the skills required of a protector."

"Then that is what I will do," Naomi said. She sat taller, staring at nothing as if she were creating a vision of the possibility for herself.

"This you must always remember," Kandake said. "The first lesson one learns in becoming a warrior is discipline. A warrior always does as she is instructed. She follows the wishes of her ruler without argument or hesitation."

Naomi's eyes widened. "Princess, I must get to the kitchens." She rushed from Kandake's rooms.

Kandake returned to the cleansing chamber and resumed her bath. This experience was far different than the first bath upon her arrival to Egypt. The women were thorough in their ministrations. They slathered her skin with a blend of aromatic creams and oils. Cleansing creams were applied to her braided hair. Kandake was warmed by the vessels of water poured over her to rinse away the creams. The temperature of the water was perfect.

The women wrung the water from her braids and wiped it from her body with large portions of softened hide. They rubbed every area of her skin with scented oil until it was well moisturized and took on a healthy glow. The servants then wrapped her hips with the fabric of her skirts and placed on her feet her cleaned, oiled sandals.

Kandake sat for them to arrange her braids and place the double-stranded necklace of lapis stones around her neck and fasten it into place. One of the women slipped the armband that represented the throne of Nubia along her arm to its proper position. When all was completed, Kandake stood refreshed and ready to attend the pharaoh's feast.

The women gathered before her and lowered themselves to their knees. The posture mirrored that of Naomi on that long ago evening when she had claimed Kandake to be Sakhmet, daughter of Ra. These servants too, held their arms raised with palms to the ceiling and heads bowed in supplication before her.

"What is this?" Kandake asked.

"Princess, we know you are the goddess." This came from the woman who had spoken of Naomi's service to Nakhtnebef. "We honor you and pledge our service to you."

"No, you are wrong. I am but the daughter of the King of Nubia." She looked from face to face, but not one of them was accepting her words.

"Princess, who else could have healed our Pharaoh of his illness, none of the healers, neither the priests could do so," she countered. "And did you not uncover and destroy the evil that had surrounded Pharaoh's throne. Tjaty would have killed Pharaoh, but you saved his life in exchange for that of the evil one, instead. These are not the deeds of a princess."

Kandake drew in a breath to argue. She intended to explain her actions taken during recent days were not of a goddess, but merely a warrior. The expressions on the faces before her said they would believe nothing less than admitting that she was Sakhmet, daughter of Ra.

47

Kandake stepped from her rooms where Shen waited to accompany her. Natasen and Alara joined them.

Needing to vent her frustration, Kandake said, "These women are convinced more than before that I am this Sakhmet."

"Little Sister, you have done some amazing things," Natasen said. The snickers of Shen and Alara reached her ears.

"Stop that, all of you," she said, rounding on them.

The group walked toward the throne room where the celebration was to be held. The servants and warriors they passed along the way either stared at Kandake in wild-eyed terror or bowed in respectful supplication.

"It seems that most have made up their minds about who you are," Alara said.

"It would appear that most have made a great mistake. I am the daughter of the king of Nubia." Kandake failed to see the humor her brothers found in this conclusion. "How am I to respond to this?"

"The same way you always do," Natasen said, as they reached the door to the celebration. "You continue to be who you are." He winked at her and walked in.

The servant at the doorway announced their arrival. Seated in attendance were the governors of Egypt's city states as well as the priests of the temple of Ptah. Everyone, including Pharaoh Nakhtnebef, stood as Kandake and her party walked to their seats. Shen took up his usual position, a few paces behind Kandake's seat.

Once she was seated the others followed suit, all except the pharaoh.

"Egypt has much to be thankful for," Nakhtnebef said, his eyes locked upon the Nubian party. "We asked for the assistance of a good friend and neighbor and were granted much more." Cheers went up throughout the room.

"Because of Nubia, Egypt was able to turn away the attack of the Assyrians. Because of Nubia, an answer to the illness of the throne of Egypt was found. Because of Nubia, an attack on the throne of Egypt was thwarted, and because of Nubia, an evil seated at the heart of Egypt was destroyed. Egypt shows its gratitude!"

A line of servants paraded into the throne room. The procession began with ten female servants. Each woman walked with outstretched arms. Upon her arms was a bolt of linen fabric and each bolt dyed a different shade of the Nubian sunset. Next, came a line of men and women bearing baskets of herbs, dates, spices, and jars of honey. Then came a line of six strong men paired in twos carrying heavy casks of gold between them.

The parade concluded with five men, each leading a pair of cows, and each one of them displayed evidence of being pregnant. "These come from Pharaoh's personal herd," Nakhtnebef said. "These are the gifts from Pharaoh Nakhtnebef of Egypt to King Amani of Nubia. May the alliance of our two kingdoms last well beyond the reigns of our children and our children's children!" This last was supported by a great out-pouring of cheers and much foot stomping.

When Nakhtnebef took his seat the food began to arrive. The pharaoh was served first. His plate and bowl were brought him by a young girl dressed in a gown of fine linen dyed the barest shade of purple. She wore a collar of jewels and circling each wrist were bracelets of gold and silver. After she had served the pharaoh, she brought plate and bowl to Prince Khabebesh.

The young girl brought plate and bowl to the honored guest of the feast, Princess Kandake. When Kandake looked into the face of the servant girl, she recognized Naomi. Her heart filled with pride as Naomi smiled back at her. A procession of servants brought in platters of food and served the remaining guests.

At the conclusion of the feasting and dismissal of the guests, a messenger of the pharaoh came to the table of the Nubian party.

"Pharaoh Nakhtnebef has requested that you meet with him in his chambers," he said.

Kandake exchanged looks with her brothers before agreeing to the invitation. They waited for the last of the guests to leave before making their way to the pharaoh..   .

"Why do you believe he has called us?" Kandake asked. "Could there be more trouble in Egypt?"

"I am not certain," Alara said. "It may be no more than the discussion of returning to Nubia with the gifts he has for Father."

"I hope that is all there is," Natasen said. "If our sister has to perform one more act as goddess, we will never be able to get her back home. The citizens will erect a temple and move her into it." Alara and Shen let loose with hoots of laughter, while Kandake swatted Natasen's arm.

48

"You called for us?" Kandake asked as their party entered the chambers of the pharaoh. Kandake felt somewhat ill at ease, Khabebesh was seated next to his father and there was a scribe sitting just behind Nakhtnebef. Whatever was to take place during this discussion, it was important enough that the pharaoh wanted it recorded.

"Yes," the pharaoh said. "Please take a seat. I have one final request of Nubia."

Kandake and the others sat in the chairs provided. The tension Kandake felt was not lessened by hearing of a new request of her father.

"Since your arrival, I have noticed a great change in Prince Khabebesh. I have spoken with him regarding this change. He says that it is due to two occurrences. The first he laid at the feet of the Princess."

Kandake searched the face of the prince, but his expression gave nothing away.

"He says, Princess, that you challenged him to speak up, make himself be heard by me and the governors of Egypt, as well. He also says that if a girl of fourteen years can rule a kingdom, then he surely can have input into ours."

Kandake worked her mouth, trying to come up with a suitable response. Nakhtnebef held up his hand for her to allow him to continue.

"The second incident that brought about the difference in the prince is one that involves Prince Alara."

Kandake turned to look at her brother.

"I have been informed that you have been tutoring my son in the layers of understanding and ruling a kingdom. He says that it was your discussion that brought him to an understanding of the history and power of this kingdom." Nakhtnebef turned in his seat and exchanged glances with the prince. "This brings me to my final request of Nubia. It is two-fold."

What more could the pharaoh want of our kingdom? Kandake brought her full attention to bear upon Nakhtnebef. *You are well, we have rid you of a usurper, and have shown you who cannot be trusted among your warriors.*

"As you are aware, Egypt is without an advisor, though he was more viper than anything else. Because of this I must attend to all matters of the kingdom until my son is able to assist me. This leaves me without time to properly train him in what he must know to rule after me." The pharaoh leaned forward in his seat and locked his gaze with Kandake's brother.

"Prince Alara, would you be willing to extend your stay here in Egypt as tutor and advisor to Prince Khabebesh for a period of time such that my son is prepared to assist me?"

"Before I give you my answer, Pharaoh Nakhtnebef, I must discuss this with Princess Kandake and consider the amount of time I will remain."

"Yes, of course," the pharaoh said. "While you are considering that I will add another thing for you to consider." He turned to Kandake. "Princess Kandake, I understand that in Nubia women get to choose what they will do, even to choose to enter training to become a warrior. My newest overseer has such a desire. She would like to follow in the foot-steps of her mother and train to become a Nubian warrior. She states that she has discussed this with you and that you have shared with her a willingness to do so."

"We have discussed this," Kandake said. "However, you have appointed her as overseer and that position requires that she remain in Egypt."

"I have at that, but I have also been thinking about the happenings of the evil in Egypt. Since the death of Naomi's mother I had chosen not to take another protector which has proved to be a mistake. Speaking with the child I realize that this is the position she aspires to and I believe that with the proper training she could fulfill that role for the throne of Egypt during my reign and that of Prince Khabebesh.

"If Prince Alara would agree to work with Prince Khabebesh, that would allow enough time for Naomi to choose and train her replacement as overseer. She could journey to Nubia when Prince Alara returns. I trust her with this task, after all it was she who discovered the cause of my illness and assisted you in my healing. I am asking this last as a special favor to the throne of Egypt."

When Nakhtnebef finished speaking, Shen whispered into Kandake's ear. She turned to face him with a questioning look. He gave her a single nod.

"We will discuss your request, Pharaoh Nakhtnebef," Kandake said. "We of Nubia have a request of our own. Shen is not only my protector, he is also the representative of the kingdom of Scythia, a recent ally of Nubia. The man you call Chatha and hold within your prison is Kuska, a Scythian warrior. He was the sworn protector of the Emissary of the Sovereign of their kingdom. He betrayed that trust, killed the Emissary, and took part in the assassination scheme against the throne of Egypt.

"Shen requests that Kuska be released to him that he may return Kuska to his Sovereign for judgment."

49

A throng of Egyptian citizens gathered before the palace of Pharaoh Nakhtnebef to see the spectacle of the caravan departing for Nubia. A wagon filled with the gifts from a grateful pharaoh stood before the palace. Behind it stamped ten healthy cows, their abdomens engorged with the young they would soon deliver. The greatest sight within this caravan was that of three contingents of Nubian warriors sitting astride strong horses with their bows slung across their backs, and Kandake and her party situated at the head of the procession. This was a far cry from the small party of Nubians that had entered the kingdom a few weeks ago.

Kandake, standing at the base of the steps leading to the palace entrance, made last minute arrangements to the saddle strapped to Strong Shadow's back. Pharaoh Nakhtnebef, who had come to send them off, stood at the top of the steps with his son, Prince

Khabebesh. Situated at their backs and positioned on either side of the two was the pharaoh's new guard. These men had been selected by the ranking Nubian and Egyptian warriors and approved by Nakhtnebef and his son. These men stood with pride and appeared to be watchful of the goings-on.

"It is almost time for us to leave," Kandake said. "Egypt is lovely, but I miss the beauty of Nubia. I am eager to return to the routine of our lives."

"Does that eagerness for your routine include your array of suitors?" Alara teased.

Kandake swatted at her brother's arm. "I will miss you," she said and embraced him. "I will even miss your need to pester me."

Alara pushed her away and held her at arm's length scrutinizing her features. "Remaining in Egypt will be difficult for me as well. I will miss you, My Queen." He lowered himself before her and bowed his head. Kandake placed her hand on the back of it conferring upon him a ruler's respect and favor.

"Do not remain in Egypt overly long," Kandake said as he rose, "I have need of you as well. After all, I depend on you to soothe me following the talks with our sister."

"I will miss you too, brother," Natasen said. "If the prince is as focused with his mind as he is with weapons training, you should not be here long." They embraced and thumped each other on the back. Natasen swung into the saddle of his mount.

"You have eased my stay away from Scythia. I await your return." Shen extended his hand and grasped the forearm of his friend. Alara returned the gesture adding a wide grin.

"Princess!" Naomi called as Kandake grasped Strong Shadow's mane and balanced to swing onto her ride.

"Naomi!" Kandake said, releasing the horse. "I feared you would not come."

"I had to finish my work before I could leave the palace. Pharaoh said that I can come to Nubia with Prince Alara when he returns."

Kandake embraced the girl and mounted her horse. She turned to see Shen approach a strange contrivance that was more cage than wagon. It contained Kuska, the traitorous Scythian warrior. Shen escorted the wagon to the center of the mounted Nubian warriors for safekeeping.

"It looks as though we are all here," Kandake said to Natasen. "Shall we begin"

Natasen raised his hand in the air and signaled for the caravan to begin their trek back to Nubia. He let loose with a shrill whistle and two warriors broke away from the host that followed. They caught up with Natasen. Kandake's brother flashed them a set of hand signals. The warriors moved ahead of the group to scout their path back to the kingdom.

The night of their first camp, Natasen assigned warriors to their watches and others to prepare their evening meal. Because the scouts' reports were negative for signs of intruders, cook fires were built.

The evening air was clear and warm. Early evening stars sparkled the darkening sky. Kandake watched as Natasen assigned the men and women to their differing duties and took reports from those who brought him information about their journey. Her heart swelled with pride as he made decisions and gave direction without hesitation.

I can see that Natasen is much more than adequate for the task, yet there is still a small part of my heart that wishes Great Mother had given the position to me.

"Princess Kandake," a voice broke into her thoughts. "I ask your pardon for interrupting you, but Prince Natasen instructed that I bring you evening meal." A warrior squatted beside her holding a dish of food.

"Thank you," she said, accepting the bowl from the warrior. "Has the prisoner been fed yet?"

"Protector Shen says that the prisoner must not eat until after all have eaten."

Kandake nodded her understanding, remembering the information Shen had given them regarding their first Scythian prisoner. When she had all but finished her meal, Natasen came to sit with her.

"I understand that Kuska is being treated as a Scythian prisoner," Kandake said. "Will that continue when we return to the kingdom?"

"That is up to Uncle Dakká," Natasen said. "Shen has great distrust for this man and is concerned that he may escape before we can get him back to Nubia."

"Is not the door locked on that cage?"

"There is no lock because there is no door into the enclosure. Shen directed that the structure be built around the man so that no one would be tempted or tricked into opening a door. He has also asked that I set watches for the day as well as the night."

"What does Shen believe Kuska to be capable of?" Kandake peered through the dark to get a better look at the man that caused her friend to use such caution. What she saw was a man in deep contemplation, not fear or desperation.

"Shen has resolved that this man should face their Sovereign and receive judgment for his crimes."

"But what of Tabiry's marriage ceremony?" Kandake asked, concern touching her voice. "If Shen returns this man to Scythia, will she not be forced to postpone all of her plans? I am grateful that I am not the one to bring her such news!"

50

Two days later, the caravan from Egypt reached the courtyard of the palace of King Amani of Nubia. King Amani, Queen Sake, and a multitude of Nubian citizens gathered around to welcome home the warriors that had gone to Egypt to assist the kingdom's ally in battle. Cheers, whistles, and musical instruments filled the air with jubilation, creating a greeting of joy and love.

Kandake dismounted and stood before her father. She was joined by Natasen and the returning warriors. As one, they lowered to one knee, crossed arms over their chests, and bowed heads offering their king the traditional position of honor and allegiance.

King Amani let his gaze rest on each person bowed before him. Then he shifted it to Shen, the caged man, and the wagon of gifts from Egypt and finally the cattle.

"Where is my son?" he asked. His voice rang throughout the courtyard.

Kandake rose from her lowered position. "My King," she said. "Prince Alara has elected to remain within Egypt for a time. He was requested to act as tutor and advisor to Prince Khabebesh."

"How long will he be gone?" Queen Sake asked. The expression of her face told all that she was not pleased. She looked to her husband. King Amani looked to Kandake.

"He says to look for him at the second waning of the moon."

"I trust the prince to do what is favorable for your reign, Princess." Her father gave a single nod of his head. "Now tell me, what are these gifts that I see? While you were away, Pharaoh Nakhtnebef had payment brought for the work of our warriors to the kingdom."

Natasen stood to give a report to the king. "Before we returned to Nubia, there was one more service that the throne was able to impart to Egypt. This is representative of Nakhtnebef's gratitude." he said. When the king gave him a questioning look, Natasen added, "The details are best reported in council."

"Very well, then." King Amani signaled for the warriors to rise and dismissed them to their families. "And the caged man?"

"That too is best held for council."

Kandake entered her rooms to refresh herself and prepare for the council meeting her father had called. She removed her dusty riding cape, the knife and the sling she wore at her side and handed these to a waiting servant. She placed her bow upon a nearby table.

It is good to be home, the familiar is always comforting. She unfastened her breastplate and once removing it passed it off to another servant.

As she walked into her cleansing chamber Tabiry's voice announced her presence.

"Why would you leave Egypt without bringing my brother home?"

It appears that all things that are familiar are not necessarily comforting. Kandake removed her skirt and stepped into the small booth before her. The women attending her, poured tall vessels of water over her travel-weary and dusty body. They slathered her skin with generous amounts of cleansers made from vegetable fats and scented with fragrant oils.

Kandake waited until her bath was complete before responding to her sister. "In the event that you are not aware, our brother became a man some time ago. This alone grants him the position of deciding whether he will leave a place or remain." She squeezed the remaining water from her braids.

"You know that I am making arrangements for my marriage ceremony. There are things I wish to discuss with him. Why would you not encourage him to return?"

Kandake looked at her sister but there were no words to improve the situation, only those that would make it worse. She chose to remain silent.

"The least you could do is have Father send a messenger to Egypt requiring Alara to come home." Tabiry folded her arms over her chest. Her eyes bored into Kandake.

"Sister, no one 'has' the king do anything. You are as capable as I. Ask Father what you would like. Besides, the date for your marriage ceremony has not been set, that is up to you." Kandake wrapped her hips with a skirt of softened hide stitched with beads of sard and went in search of small meal.

From the kitchen, Kandake received a dish of spicy stew. It contained chunks of meat, small onions, and a good helping of grain, all of this covered by a thick sauce. She took the bowl to the steps at the back of the palace. There she sat to replenish her body after the long journey and to sort through her thoughts. Discussing the problems of Tabiry's plans brought to mind a few of her own.

I am not prepared to marry, but bouncing from one suitor to another is not to my liking. It confuses me. It builds relationships that I have little to no intention to continue. She looked out over the land, watching the people come and go, attending to their daily errands. Those who noticed her sitting there nodded in recognition of her status.

What Nubia requires of me is strength and wisdom. Whether I choose a husband or not the requirement remains the same. She tore off a piece of bread, scooped a portion of the stew with it, and filled her mouth. *I will do what must be done in the way that fits this queen. I will choose a husband, but our marriage date will be set for a time that is suitable to what I need most.* She took another mouthful of her meal. The flavors matched her emotions and determination—strong and resolute.

To rule Nubia well I must be all of the things Great Mother sees within me, these are the qualities that must grow and flourish. The man I choose as husband must recognize these things in me and appreciate them. Beyond this, he must have an uncompromising love for children.

Just then a small child broke away from her mother and ran to the steps where Kandake sat. The seeds and thick juice of a honeyed fig smeared across her face.

"I missed you Princess," the child said. "Mother said that you were on a journey and would not be back for a long time, but I saved my treat for you." She pulled the remains of an old, squashed, half-eaten, sweetened fruit from a cloth sack she carried. She thrust it at Kandake with a smile that said she was presenting Kandake with the world's greatest treasure.

"Thank you," she said with a smile to match the child's. Kandake searched the sad treat for a clean spot she could pinch a small bit to eat. Succeeding at finding the lone place, she nipped the morsel, put it in her mouth and swallowed without chewing. She refused to think about the times that fruit had been dragged through the dust.

The pleasure beaming from the child's face from Kandake eating the fruit was exceeded by the pride in her mother's expression. "Thank you, Princess." Was all she said as she scooped up the girl and continued on her way.

I cannot be the only one eating old, dusty treats. This thought came to her as she returned to the task of sorting through her suitors. *Semna and Irike are good men. One is generous, the other hard working, and both are kind. These are qualities that are good for Nubia, but I require more. Amhara has strength and is forward-looking in all his plans. Nesiptah is patient and his company is soothing. The qualities of both of these men will serve Nubia well and both are more than suitable to my desires. Yet, one is more....*

Kandake took the last bite of her meal and with it things became more clear about whom she would choose. All that was left was to inform each of them.

_51_

Kandake sat next to her father in the council chamber. None the others had arrived yet.

"Father, why did you present yourself to Mother?" she asked.

"Your mother was not only the most beautiful woman in the kingdom, she was also the most intelligent and hard working. She was much like you."

"How do you mean?" Kandake chose a honeyed fig from the plate in the center of the table.

"She was reluctant to accept suitors and when at last she did, she only received a few. I was fortunate to have been one of them. Your mother had apprenticed to the kingdom's healer and used her time to study and grow herbs and medicinal plants."

"Our mother was preparing to become a healer?" Kandake asked. "And she abandoned her training to become your queen? It is difficult for me to believe our mother would discard anything that was important to her."

"She would not." King Amani took hold of his daughter's hand. "You and your mother share the same determination. She would not turn her back on becoming a healer any more than you would relinquish your dream of becoming a warrior."

"When you were ill mother refused to leave your side."

"To care for me when the healer could not and to be sure I received all that I required."

"Is that why she oversees the stores of frankincense and other medicines?" Kandake asked.

"And meets with the kingdom's healers to discuss not only what supplies they might need but to monitor the health of the kingdom."

Kandake was quiet. Her gaze dropped to the table top. She could not face her father because of the sadness she felt for her mother. *It appears in this family I am not the only one to sacrifice their dreams for the kingdom.*

"Why the sadness in your eyes?" her father asked.

"If Mother had chosen to marry another, she would have been able to become the healer she wanted."

"Your mother chose to marry me so that she could become the healer she desired to be. Had she married another, she would have cared for only a few people at a time. As queen of Nubia, your mother cares for the entire kingdom."

Kandake studied her father's face. The pride he felt for his wife was evident in his eyes. The more she thought of her mother's choice to marry her father the more clear things became. Her mind reflected to the conversations she had had with Great Mother, Aunt Alodia, and her mother about how to choose a husband from among her suitors. In this moment Kandake knew she had made the correct decision. *I know what is best for me and for this kingdom. I will make my choice and it will serve both!*

Aunt Alodia and Uncle Naqa came into the room and took their seats at the table. Soon after, Tabiry entered, followed by Natasen and Uncle Dakká. The meeting of the council began.

"Prince Natasen, please give your report regarding the return of our warriors," King Amani said.

Natasen described the circumstances he discovered surrounding the request for the retention of Nubia's warriors in Egypt. He informed the king of the warriors' suspicions that they were asked to remain for reasons other than to maintain peace within Egypt.

"And what of the pharaoh's distress symbol?" the king asked.

Kandake gave the report. "Your concerns were correct," she said, and went on to tell of the pharaoh being poisoned and the advisor's plans to usurp the throne of Egypt.

"So that is where the gift comes in," King Amani said. "But what of the man in the cage?"

"That is best told by Shen," Natasen said. "His report will not only answer that question but a few more regarding the attackers along the trade routes."

King Amani instructed a messenger to call Shen to the council chamber. When the Scythian arrived, he was seated at the foot of the table and told the king about his prisoner.

"King Amani, with your permission I will start at the beginning of this account," Shen said. "As you recall I became known to Princess Kandake during the rescue of Prince Alara. It was believed that he had been responsible for the death of the Emissary of the Sovereign of Scythia. We know that he is innocent of that offence. In Egypt I found the true assassin, Kuska. It was he who was responsible for that meaningless death as well as the attacks upon your caravans." He asked for a bowl of water and drank it down. He clenched his fists and continued.

"It was his plan to take possession of the Sovereign's ironstone and present himself to the kingdoms as the representative of Scythia and solicit gifts and alliances with the rulers of these lands. With these riches and bonds he would build his own kingdom. His plans went awry when the stone became lost.

"This forced him to abandon that plan and he began robbing those who ventured along the trade routes. As evil men learn of other evil men, he came to the attention of Tjaty Herihor and his desire to sit on the throne of Egypt. He traded his knowledge and skill as an assassin for a position of prominence when Herihor came to power. I am certain that the man, Herihor, would not have lived long upon that throne."

"If I may, My King?" Uncle Dakká said. The king nodded his permission. "Why bring this man to Nubia?"

"It is my duty to return the assassin to Scythia where he can face the judgment of the Sovereign. Nubia has the only warriors equal to the task of guarding the assassin until I am prepared to make the journey."

_52_

"You knew Shen was preparing to return to Scythia, why did you not tell me?" Tabiry spat the words at Kandake. She shook with rage.

"He is your chosen," Kandake said. "It is his place to say this to you."

"You planned this! You had Shen wait to tell me just before he told the council so that we would not have time to discuss the matter."

"I did no such thing," Kandake said. "When Shen told you was his choice, not mine. We had no discussion." Kandake worked to keep her voice calm and not allow her sister to provoke her into an argument.

"This is all your doing! First you have Alara remain in Egypt and then you talk Shen into leaving the kingdom, just so that my marriage ceremony can be postponed!" She burst into tears.

Kandake had seen her sister upset many times. In fact Tabiry was often upset to the point of wild accusations and tears, but this time was something different. It put her in mind of the time when Alara went missing. It was true that Tabiry could annoy the teeth from a crocodile, but she loved her sister.

"Sister, why must your plans change?"

"Because I wanted all of my family to attend the ceremony," she sobbed. "And Shen desires to make the journey to Scythia as soon as possible to avoid harsh weather during his travels. Now I will have to wait until he returns and I am not certain how long that will be."

Kandake dipped a bit of cloth into a pitcher of water. With it she cleaned her sister's face. "There is another solution. Would you be willing to have a guest from another kingdom participate in your ceremony?"

ço cz

Kandake sat on the bench just outside the sparing floor of the warriors' compound. She wiped her skin with a dampened piece of hide, mopping away the perspiration of a long, intricate drill set by Uncle Dakká.

"Your movement is smooth and even," Amhara said, sitting down beside her.

"Thank you, I am still thinking about the footwork." Kandake said. "I know my focus should be on the attack, but when I do my feet misstep and my balance is off."

"You know as with all moves, this one too comes with much practice. That pass took me many days of countless sessions to master."

"Then there is hope for me yet." She flashed him a smile. "I understand that Ezena will be returning to practice in the morning. Perhaps she is available for a visit this afternoon. Would you care to come along with me?" The smile on his face and the light in his eyes gave her the answer before he said that he would join her.

"I understand that this warrior Shen has brought from Egypt is supposed to be very dangerous," Amhara said. He returned the weapons he had used during his practice to their places.

"He is more than a warrior, he is an assassin. Not only is he skillful in battle, he is quite knowledgeable in poisons and sly with words." Kandake deposited the hide she had used in the basket to be cleaned.

"That would explain the reason that only senior warriors are assigned to guard him." He looked around the room as if seeking something to continue their conversation. "I have not been idle while you were away."

"I would not expect that of you," Kandake said, walking toward the exit of the building. "I must return to the palace. Great Mother and I are sharing afternoon meal. Afterwards, I will be walking to visit Ezena."

"May I walk with you to the palace?" Amhara asked. When Kandake accepted his company, Amhara folded his hands behind his back and walked alongside her maintaining an adequate distance that their bodies would not touch. As there was no one with them to post shield, it was important he adhere to the utmost in propriety.

"What has kept you occupied while I was away?" she asked.

"I have laid the foundation to the home I said I would build. If there is time following our visit to Ezena, I would like for you to see it."

"That would be a pleasant walk," she said. They arrived at the entrance to the palace and arranged the time for their visit with Ezena.

Kandake walked through the corridors of the palace. She stopped in the kitchens to acquire the tray of food that she would share with her grandmother. When she reached Great Mother's doorway, Kandake lowered to her knees exhibiting the respect she felt for the woman.

"There you are," Great Mother said. "I have been looking forward to this visit. Sit here next to me." Great Mother patted the large pillow beside her. Kandake sat down, setting the tray of food on the low table in front of them.

"You have brought my favorites," her grandmother said. "I can always count on a special treat from you. Now tell me what you have been thinking."

"I have been considering many things, Great Mother, but what has been on my mind most is the kingdom of Nubia and what the future will bring to it under my rule." She served a plate for her grandmother and one for herself. Kandake gave Great Mother an extra serving of the tiny onions she so enjoyed. They had been gathered this morning and

Kandake knew they would snap and crunch as her grandmother chewed them—just the way she liked.

"What do you mean?" Great Mother asked. She popped one of the onions into her mouth.

"The events of our visit to Egypt opened my eyes to the importance of trust and loyalty of the ones who advise you. As queen I will have my family as council and each of them loves this kingdom as much as I do. And when I choose a husband he must not only love Nubia, he must be willing to serve it in every way possible, as well as be a comfort and true support to me." She took a bite of the food before her and gazed through the window.

The kingdom she loved stretched before her view as its people walked to and fro, going about their daily concerns. There were herdsmen, craftsmen, mothers, fathers, and children. It is family that makes Nubia what it is. Everyone doing what was needful to not just sustain their lives, but to take joy in the relationships around them. It delighted her heart to take it in. *I will protect this with my life!*

"While I am not prepared to take a husband today, I have made my choice and will tell him soon."

"And will you tell me?" Great Mother smiled at Kandake. The joy in her eyes matched her broad grin.

53

    Kandake and Amhara walked to the area where Nateka and Ezena had built their home, Kashta and Nedjeh followed a short distance behind, posting shield. As they approached, Nateka could be heard in his workshop pounding metal.

    "Hello," Amhara called through the doorway. "Are you receiving visitors?"

    "Amhara!" Nateka said, putting aside the piece he had been working. He wiped his hands on his apron and embraced Amhara. "Ezena said that we would have visitors when word got out that she was returning to the warriors' compound. It is good to see you." As he walked through the doorway, he noticed Kandake and sketched a quick bow.

    "You are the husband of my dear friend," Kandake said. "It is my hope to make many visits to your home. If you bow every time I see you, you will get nothing done and Ezena will complain that you have become lazy." They laughed as Ezena joined them.

"What are you laughing about?" she asked looking from face to face.

"Princess Kandake was just remarking how I do not work enough to provide for you," Nateka teased.

"That is not what I said," Kandake said. "I was remarking that if Nateka bowed every time I came around he would not get his work done."

"Did you not say that he was lazy?" Amhara said, continuing the teasing.

"I do believe she said something about my being lazy."

The more Kandake attempted to explain herself, the more Nateka and Amhara continued to tease her. The four laughed loud and hard. Kandake wrapped her arms around her middle, the laughter causing spasms in her overworked muscles.

"I understand that you are returning to the compound for practice tomorrow," Kandake said to her friend in an attempt to change the subject. "It will be good to see you again."

"It is true. I will be there early in the morning," Ezena said. "Come inside, I would like to show you what Nateka has crafted for our home." She took hold of Kandake's hand and the two went inside leaving Amhara with Nateka.

Kandake crossed the threshold into her friend's home. The walls were made of red-brown brick fashioned from the mud of the area and baked to a durable hardness. The floor was covered with the same mud bricks. Heavy, woven fabric hung from the wall on the long side of the room. The dyed threads of the weave formed a scene portraying herdsman driving several cows.

Kandake studied the depiction made from a meticulous weave of woolen yarn. "The work is beautiful. Whichever artisan did this possesses great talent."

"It is the work of Nateka's sister. It is a gift to celebrate our marriage. But that is not what I brought you in to see." She led her friend toward the back of the house.

"Look at this, is not my husband the most wonderful craftsman?" Ezena handed Kandake a basket made of woven strands of iron. "This is so that I can carry hot coals from his workshop to the oven to prepare our meals. And this." She passed Kandake a sheet of copper framed in iron scrollwork. The copper sheet had been polished to a very smooth surface. Kandake was able to see her reflection to near fine detail.

"It is beautiful," Kandake said. She and Ezena sat on low benches within the room. "You appear to be very happy. I cannot recall seeing you express such joy."

"I cannot describe what I feel. I am more than content. What about you? Tell me about your suitors. Has my cousin proven worthy?"

"Before I left for Egypt I was confused about the choice I should make. Each of my suitors possessed different traits and I could see great benefit in choosing them. As I can only choose one, how should I choose? I sought wisdom from Great Mother, and

Aunt Alodia. Each gave me different answers, even my mother's answer confused me." Kandake faced her friend. It had been too long since the friends had shared their hearts.

"In that kingdom a situation occurred in which I was forced to know who I am and what my life as queen must be. That is when it became clear to me the husband I would need to live that life. I know who I will choose for my husband."

"Who have you told?" Ezena asked, excitement exploding from her. "You must tell me."

"I have yet to tell my mother, but I will tell you." She leaned forward and whispered the name into her friend's ear.

"I knew it!" Ezena squealed. "When will you tell him?"

"After I have told my family."

54

Three weeks following Kandake's return from
Egypt she stood in the center of the throne room.
Tables and benches had been brought in for the family
meal that would precede the marriage ceremony of her
sister. Tabiry fluttered from one thing and then to
another making sure that all of the arrangements
would be just the way she had wanted.

"Here they are, my sisters!" Alara's voice boomed
within the room.

"You are here!" Tabiry squealed. She ran to her
brother and embraced him. "I feared you would not
arrive." She released him becoming aware that others
stood with him. She stared at first the one and then the
other.

"Princess Tabiry," Alara said. "I would like you to
meet Prince Khabebesh, son of Nakhtnebef, Pharaoh
of Egypt. I told the pharaoh that I could not miss my
sister's wedding ceremony and suggested that it would

be good for the prince to gain knowledge of the land of his ally to the south. There is no better way to gain an understanding of Nubia than through the kingdom's greatest celebration!"

Tabiry examined the young man from head to foot. The red tint of his brown skin boasted his heritage of the land to the north. "Thank you for coming," she said. Her gaze shifted to the second person with Alara. "And who is this?"

"I am Naomi," she said. "I am here to train to become a warrior." Naomi turned her gaze upon Kandake. "Princess, I am here! Pharaoh allowed me to come early. I have been training Subira. She is good at preparation, but she must learn to keep her eyes up. I tell her to watch everything. Sometimes she forgets and shifts her gaze to the floor when nobles come near." The words spilled from Naomi's lips like a rushing stream whose dam has been overflowed.

Kandake and Alara laughed. "She has been like this since she became overseer. She spoke without ceasing throughout the journey home."

"That is not so." Naomi glared at him, but there was no true malice it in.

"I must agree with the little one," Khabebesh said. Naomi flashed him a grin. "There were times when my father's overseer fell asleep."

Kandake and the others laughed, even Naomi joined in.

"I am told that I have a new student entering the compound, and possibly a second," Uncle Dakká said, entering the throne room. He came to stand with the small group, but his eyes were riveted to the young girl.

"Prince Dakká, I present to you Prince Khabebesh of Egypt," Alara said.

"It is good to meet the son of Nubia's ally." Uncle Dakká's gaze met that of the prince but bounced back to Naomi. He lowered himself to his knees to greet the child face to face. "Irty," he whispered.

"You know my mother?" Naomi said.

"I would know her face anywhere," he said. He wrapped his arms about the child. "Tell me, is she well?"

"My mother died four years ago, great sir." The information appeared to cause Uncle Dakká great sadness.

"Uncle, you knew Naomi's mother?" Kandake asked.

"Irty left the kingdom many years ago. She was one of our best warriors. I would have presented myself as suitor, but she believed that to take a husband would distract her from what she desired most. When she advanced to senior status, Irty took her skills to Egypt and became Protector of the Pharaoh." He embraced Naomi a second time

As he stood, Uncle Dakká directed his attention to Prince Khabebesh. "I understand that it is your wish to train with our warriors. In the time that you have within Nubia, we will see what you are able to learn."

"Thank you Prince Dakká, training here will be a great honor," the prince said, "I am certain I will learn much during my stay. But my father's overseer is the one who is to train. She desires to become a great warrior and ultimately the Protector of the throne of Egypt, just as her mother."

Uncle Dakká's face took on the likeness of stone. He turned from the prince to gaze upon Naomi. Tears overflowed his eyes and ran, unhindered, down his cheeks. "This student I will train myself."

55

Members of Kandake's family poured into the throne room. Seats were taken and conversations began. The roar of laughter filled the room as remembrances and stories were told throughout the meal.

Naomi and Prince Khabebesh were seated at the table with Alara and Kandake as their guests. Natasen sat at the table with Shen who had no family to accompany him. But his table was far from empty. Shen had invited Ezena and Nateka and several other warriors he had come to know and they brought their families.

Kandake visited the table to express her pleasure and to welcome Shen into the family. "It is good to know that my sister will bring strong children into our family," she said. "It is my hope that having a husband that is a warrior will enrich my sister's understanding that things are not always as we wish them to be."

Great Mother joined those at Shen's table. She exchanged her seat with another to sit with him. "I am pleased," Great Mother said. "My granddaughter has chosen well."

"It is my hope that she has," Shen said. "I am a warrior. I have grown accustomed to life being difficult, with few luxuries at hand. Now I will be wed to one who has not known such rough living. What am I to do when things are not as she wishes them to be?"

"The same as the rest of us have done," Great Mother said. "When Tabiry is displeased or frustrated, she rants, screeches, and often wails her displeasure. We, who are around her, have learned to wait out the storm. Allow the winds to blow, they will soon cease. Then we present to her the options that are available and leave it at that."

"Would it not be better to present these choices before the storm blows?" he asked.

"Dear Scythian, when have you ever known it to prosper any man to stand against the wind? The danger is always that he may get blown away." Great Mother returned to her table.

Shen considered her words after she had gone. He had long admired the older woman's gracious manner and wise reflections.

"By this time tomorrow I will call you brother," Kandake said.

"And I will have achieved that which I never believed possible," Shen said. "I will have a beautiful wife who cares for me."

Kandake was taken aback by the tenderness expressed by the warrior. She had seen many sides to

Shen, but this one was a pleasant surprise. "Have you removed your belongings from the warrior compound?"

"Yes, I will be sleeping this night in Prince Natasen's rooms. He and Amhara insisted that returning to the quiet of the compound after this celebration would fill my heart with loneliness. They declared this to be a night a man must spend with his family, a time to discuss the ways of marriage and understand how to care for his wife."

"Neither of them has a wife!" Kandake exclaimed. Her voice carried throughout the room drawing the attention of her parents. She smiled and waved them back to their conversations.

"Amhara tells me that he has been discussing the subject with the elders of the kingdom. He has gained much wisdom. It is his desire to be chosen as husband." Shen gave Kandake a pointed look.

As the night waned, those attending the celebration began to leave to prepare for tomorrows ceremony. Kandake returned to her original seat across from her parents. Tabiry and Shen sat alone at a table in deep conversation.

Although I never would have imagined such a match, Kandake thought gazing at the couple, *they look good together, well paired.*

"Why is it taking so long for my children to marry?" Queen Sake said to her husband.

"I do not know," King Amani said. "My sons have yet to present themselves and our other daughter has just begun to receive suitors. If that process develops anything like that of her sister, it could be a long time before she makes a choice."

Kandake giggled at their exaggerated sighs of long suffering. "It may help my brother if he understood more about marriage and the ways to care for a wife."

"Alara has his eye on someone? He has spoken to you?" King Amani leaned forward, every line of his body hopeful.

"I believe that to be true, but I was speaking of Natasen." Kandake watched with glee as the eyes of her parents bulged, staring at her.

"Who is the woman," her mother asked.

"Never mind the woman, why does Natasen need this conversation?" her father insisted.

"It is not Natasen that requires the information," Kandake said, pointedly ignoring her mother's question. "It is Shen. He has no family here, so he is sleeping the night in Natasen's rooms. He and Amhara intend to have that discussion with him. I suggested that it would be wise to have this conversation with someone who actually has a wife."

The king and queen of Nubia burst into laughter. They turned to look first at Tabiry and Shen, then turned to look at their son, Natasen, and laughed again. "What was that you were saying about Alara?" her mother asked.

"It is not proper that I tell you that which my brother is not ready to make known. Let it be enough that he may be interested in presenting himself."

Her parents quibbled and cajoled in an attempt to get Kandake to give them the information they sought.

"How do you expect us to sleep tonight with such a question on our hearts," Queen Sake said.

"Can you not sleep well knowing that your daughter will take her husband tomorrow, one who is honorable and strong?" Kandake teased, looking again at Tabiry and Shen.

"We have other children," King Amani said. "It is a parent's duty to see to the care of all of them." He put on such a pitiful face, Kandake's heart was touched. When her mother took on a similar expression, she felt for them.

"Then I will tell you something." The expressions on their faces changed from forlorn to that of eagerness with such speed, Kandake broke into a fit of giggles. "I will not tell you about my brother, but I will say something about myself. I have chosen!"

_56_

The morning of Tabiry's marriage ceremony was clear and bright. Her mother woke early to braid her hair. The style was intricate and gemstone beads were interwoven among the plaits adding depth and beauty.

Kandake wrapped a skirt of fine linen about her sister's hips. The fabric had been dyed a deep midnight blue. Seed-like beads of gold had been sewn about the fabric mimicking the look of lapis lazuli, the gemstone that was the seal of the kingdom of Nubia. The length of the skirt draped from Tabiry's waist to dust the tops of her feet.

From her neck to just below her collarbone hung a double strand of beads alternating between the lapis of Nubia and perfectly formed orbs of pure gold, each was twin in size and shape to the one next to it.

Kandake dusted her sister's eyelids with gold she had powdered herself and then outlined her eyes in attractive lines of kohl.

When the ministrations were completed, servants carried a large piece of reflective copper into the room and placed it before Tabiry.

"Is that me?" she asked. "Thank you so much, you have made me beautiful!" She embraced her mother and then Kandake. It was the first time in a very long while, if ever, that Kandake remembered her sister appreciating and admiring anything she had done.

∽ ∾

A loud thumping occurred at the palace doors. It sounded again. On the third pounding, guards opened the doors.

"I have come for my wife, Tabiry, the daughter of King Amani," Shen spoke the traditional words. He also presented her father with a customary bride price. He offered a cow, two goats, gifts of ironworks, and a small bag of gold.

King Amani placed Tabiry's hand into Shen's. He led her down the palace steps and walked with her out of the courtyard gates. Because they would be living in the palace, Shen led her once around the outside of the enclosure and back to the entrance to her rooms that had just been built into the outer wall of the palace.

Shen guided Tabiry inside while he remained in the doorway and answered the ceremonial questions of protection asked by the priest. Once every part of the ceremony had been fulfilled, Tabiry and Shen walked inside their new residence and closed the door. At this point a Nubian warrior came and stood guard at the entrance, armed with bow, knife, and sling—a representation to all that this union was approved by King Amani of Nubia and had received his blessing.

<u>57</u>

Tabiry's marriage ceremony at an end, King Amani opened the courtyard to the citizens of Nubia to join in the celebration. Tables were set in all of the available space of the area. Servants brought platters of roasted meats, cheeses, sliced fruits, and breads that covered the tabletops. Pitchers of water and mixed fruit juices were in great supply. Platters of honeyed figs, dates, and pomegranates were circulated on the shoulders of servants.

"Our sister is married," Alara said. He took a sip from the bowl of the mixed juice he held.

"From the look of things, Prince Khabebesh may be reluctant to return to Egypt," Kandake said, observing the way the prince enjoyed the company of those around him.. "How long will the two of you remain in Nubia?"

"We must leave within a few days," Alara said.

"You have journeyed a long distance to remain only a few days. Must you hurry back? I am certain there is much the prince can learn in Nubia that would serve him as ruler."

"Pharaoh Nakhtnebef postponed a few items of business so that I could attend our sister's marriage ceremony. An important item is to be discussed within the council Nakhtnebef has called with his governors. Prince Khabebesh must be in attendance. The pharaoh is anxious to dispel the opinion of the prince's weakness and immaturity that Herihor created." Kandake nodded. "That is the reason the prince and I must return so soon. Otherwise I would have extended our visit."

Alara appeared to be staring at something behind Kandake. She turned her head to see what had captured her brother's attention. It was the young woman they had passed on their walk some weeks ago, Nedjeh's cousin. When he realized Kandake was watching him, he shifted his gaze back to her.

"You are not taking Naomi with you?" Kandake asked. She searched the crowded area for the young girl. She found her in the company of her cousin, Kheb. The girls were similar in age and size. They had their heads together chattering and giggling about something it appeared that only the two of there were privy to.

"No," Alara said. "She has chosen to remain in Nubia. She will live here and train until she advances to the rank of senior. Then it will be up to her whether she will return to Egypt. If she so chooses."

"Would she not be required to do as the pharaoh ordered?" she asked.

"I had almost forgotten," Alara said. "Nakhtnebef requested I give you this." He pulled a rolled sheet of papyrus from within his robe. It was affixed with the seal of the pharaoh of Egypt.

Kandake took it from her brother, removed the seal and began reading:

Princess Kandake,

I am grateful for all that you have done for the kingdom of Egypt. Yet, I have one more request to make. As you know, Naomi's mother, Irty, was a citizen of Nubia. She became wed to a Hebrew whose freedom she purchased prior to marrying him. That makes the birth of her child, Naomi, a free born citizen of Nubia. At Irty's death, it was her desire that her child grow to become a woman within Nubia. She believed this would be better than becoming a woman in this kingdom. I fear that I must agree with her. Naomi would never be allowed to develop the spirit her mother had here in Egypt. This, Irty requested of me and to my shame I have neglected this promise. In my defense

I confess that I enjoyed the child's strong spirit, so much like her mother's, I could not bear to send her away.

It is Naomi's desire to become a true Nubian warrior. That is a thing that would not be possible if she were to remain in Egypt or become one of its citizens. So I am sending her to you.

I ask that you would see to her training and provide for her. Allow her to become educated in schooling and the ways of Nubian culture. I will, with great eagerness, finance and supply anything she needs or whatever you require.

As you do this, the throne of Egypt will be indebted to you always.

The letter ended with the same symbol Pharaoh Nakhtnebef had used when requesting the aid of her father.

"What is it?" Alara asked. "Your face carries the look of a troubled mother."

"That may be because I have just become that."

58

"Is there a problem?" Alara asked. "Has something happened in Egypt?"

"No," Kandake said. "It has happened here. I must find Father."

Kandake wove her way through the throng of celebrants looking for her father. She found King Amani laughing and enjoying the afternoon with his siblings. She stood by his side waiting for an opportunity to interrupt. She touched his arm.

"Father, I must speak with you and Mother." She begged the pardon of her aunt and uncles and the three of them stepped into the throne room, away from the crowd.

"It appears Egypt has one more request of the throne of Nubia," she said after the door was sealed. She handed the letter from Pharaoh Nakhtnebef to her parents. They read it.

"Are you willing to do this?" her mother asked. "It is a huge responsibility. All of my children have grown. I would not mind...."

"Nakhtnebef asked this of me and I already have a relationship with the child." Kandake stood thinking. Her expression took on the faraway look of one pondering weighty issues. She came to a decision. "Last night I told you that I had chosen the man to become my husband. This does not change that. However, if I am to take this on, he must have the opportunity to decide if he would have this as part of his life."

"You would marry now?" Queen Sake asked.

"No. It was my decision to choose now, but to marry later—that has not changed." She looked from her mother to her father. "I would like to make the announcement of my choice and this development to the people of Nubia."

"As you wish," her father said.

King Amani opened the doors to the throne room and walked out onto the portico. He took the hand of his wife and stepped forward to make his announcement.

"I, King Amani of Nubia, along with Queen Sake have an announcement to make," he bellowed.

The courtyard fell silent. All eyes turned toward him.

"Princess Kandake, future queen of Nubia, is prepared to announce the name of her chosen."

Kandake joined her parents on the portico. "Citizens of Nubia, this day my sister Princess Tabiry has taken a husband and we all celebrate that occasion.

It means that before too long the greatest resource of this kingdom will increase. May they bless Nubia with strong children." Cheers went up from the crowd.

"The day has come for me to think of the future and that includes all of you. I have chosen the man to spend that future with, Amhara, journeyman warrior of Nubia." More cheers and whistles filled the air.

With a grin as wide as the Nile river is long, Amhara made his way to the portico to stand beside Kandake. He extended his had to confirm his agreement.

"Before you agree," Kandake said. "There is something you must know. Pharaoh Nakhtnebef, ruler of Egypt, has asked that I become mother to a child sent to live in this kingdom." Her gaze panned the crowd looking for the young girl. She spotted Naomi standing next to her new-found friend, Kheb. "Naomi, would you come stand with me please," she called.

"Naomi, I received a letter from the pharaoh of Egypt. He says that your mother requested that you grow to womanhood in Nubia. Since you are a free born child, you have that right. He also asked that I become your new mother in place of Irty, whom we have lost. Do you understand these things?"

"Yes," Naomi said.

"And do you agree with these things?"

"Princess does that mean that I get to live with you?" When Kandake nodded her head, Naomi said, "Yes! Yes!"

"Then before the citizens of Nubia, I adopt Naomi as my daughter. Therefore all rights and privileges that passed to me as daughter of King Amani of Nubia, I now pass to my daughter, Naomi."

The citizens standing around the portico went wild. Cheers, stomping of feet, the pounding of one another's backs was without restraint. Kandake waited for the noise to die away before she continued.

"Amhara, I have chosen you to become my husband, but I now have a daughter. If you accept my choice you also agree that Naomi is your daughter with all of the rights and privileges of future children that would come of our marriage."

Amhara knelt before Naomi. "I will make a good father. I am a hard worker and a warrior. I promise to provide for you and protect you with all that I am. If you allow me I would like that honor."

With wide eyes, Naomi nodded yes.

Amhara stood and faced Kandake. "Princess Kandake, if you will take my hand, I will provide for you, I will protect you, and I will be a good father to all of our children."

He held his left hand out to Kandake and his right hand out to Naomi. Kandake laid her hand upon his. Amhara took hold of it and brought it to his lips, sealing their commitment to each other. Naomi laid her hand upon his. He took hold of it and brought it to his lips.

The people of Nubia cheered harder than before, stomping the ground and pounding one another without end. King Amani attempted to quiet them but it was no use. He would have to wait until they ended on their own.

Kandake's heart soared. She would marry the man she loved and admired and would raise the daughter she had come to love and respect.

If you enjoyed *Warrior of the Egyptian Kingdom* be sure to tell a friend, leave a review on Amazon.com or Smashwords.com or wherever you'd like to spread the news!

Don't forget to keep a look out for the next adventures of the Princess Kandake series, *A Journey Undertaken*

ABOUT THE AUTHOR

Stephanie Jefferson loves all forms of story – oral, written, cinematic, and any other form you can think of. She says she writes because of the way it makes her brain feel. Her greatest desire is to craft a story that the reader never wants to end.

Stephanie lives is Prescott Valley, AZ with her husband and gets bossed around by her 17lb terrier, Mr. Jenkins.

Places she can be found
Website: http://stephaniejefferson.com/
Facebook:https://www.facebook.com/pages/Stephanie-Jefferson/111146985571699
Twitter: @StephaniePQW

Send her a message:
stephanie@stephaniejefferson.com. She's waiting to hear from you.

18903700R00160